TALES OF
Don Quixote

TALES OF
Don Quixote

RETOLD BY BARBARA NICHOL

Tundra Books

Published in Canada by Tundra Books,
481 University Avenue, Toronto, Ontario M5G 2E9

Published in the United States by Tundra Books of Northern New York,
P.O. Box 1030, Plattsburgh, New York 12901

Library of Congress Control Number: 2004103920

National Library of Canada Cataloguing in Publication

Nichol, Barbara (Barbara Susan Lang)
    Tales of Don Quixote / retold by Barbara Nichol.

ISBN 0-88776-674-9

    1. Don Quixote (Fictitious character) – Juvenile fiction.
2. Spain – Juvenile fiction. I. Title.

PS8577.I165T34 2004   JC813'.54   C2004-902035-8

We acknowledge the financial support of the Government of Canada
through the Book Publishing Industry Development Program and that of the
Government of Ontario through the Ontario Media Development
Corporation's Ontario Book Initiative. We further acknowledge the support
of the Canada Council for the Arts and the Ontario Arts Council for our
publishing program.

Design: Cindy Elisabeth Reichle
Printed and bound in Canada

This book is printed on acid-free paper that is 100% recycled,
ancient-forest friendly (100% post-consumer recycled).

1 2 3 4 5 6   09 08 07 06 05 04

For my friend Bill Richardson

Acknowledgments

I started this book after making a radio documentary on *Don Quixote* for CBC Radio's "Ideas" series. The shows involved almost two years of interviews and conversations with scholars whose names will be very familiar to anyone who has studied Cervantes. They are A.J. Close, Barry Ife, Diana de Armas Wilson, Carroll B. Johnson, James Iffland, James Parr, Donald McCrory, Burton Raffel, Daniel Eisenberg, Eduardo Urbina, Edward H. Friedman, and Maria Antonia Garcés. I am so grateful for their time and insights.

I read a number of translations and editions of *Don Quixote* in preparing to write this: among them the very highly regarded new translations by Burton Raffel, John Rutherford, and Edith Grossman and the classic translations by Tobias Smollett, Walter Starkie, Charles Jarvis, and John Ormsby.

Many thanks to Bernie Lucht at CBC Radio, to Barry Moser, and to Kong Njo, Tamara Sztainbok, Kathryn Cole, and – once again – Kathy Lowinger at Tundra Books.

PROLOGUE

Miguel de Cervantes wrote a prologue to the first volume of his great book *The Ingenious Gentleman Don Quixote of la Mancha* explaining that he couldn't seem to write a proper prologue. He couldn't think of something good enough to say. He tells us he spent hours stymied at his desk. When his prologue ends, he hasn't even found a way to start.

This is how the book begins. A book about his hero and also about writing his big book about his hero, Don Quixote – an ordinary man who thinks he is a knight.

When it first came out, *Don Quixote* was a surprise to readers – not like any books they'd read before. That was four hundred years ago. And even now, literature is borrowing ideas from Cervantes and trying to catch up.

The world Cervantes describes in *Don Quixote* is a kaleidoscope, a hall of mirrors, different every time you turn around, different seen through every pair of eyes. Don't be too sure of anything, Cervantes seems to say.

To make this point, he pretends he didn't write this book at all. He tells us that he found the stories of Quixote and only had the first part when he started out. He had to hunt around to find the rest. You'll see.

We don't know much about Cervantes. We think he was a soldier at one time, and very brave. He lost the use of one of his hands in a battle on the sea. He was captured once by pirates and spent five years in jail in northern Africa.

We know Cervantes loved to read and loved to write, but all his life had other jobs to make a living. For years he traveled back and forth across Spain, collecting provisions for the campaigns of the crown. He was jailed twice – unfairly so it seems – for business scrapes that could not be avoided. He was excommunicated by the church. The church was not always cooperative when it came to paying taxes to the crown. He was almost sixty by the time he wrote his masterpiece.

He published *Don Quixote* in 1604. It made him very famous. This is the book I'm retelling here. And then a decade later he wrote Book Two.

Now, why retell *Don Quixote?*

The work is very long and very old. The book that you are holding is a shortcut, until the day arrives when you might find the time and place to read the work in full.

I've left a few things out in the retelling. For the most part they are stories that don't involve Quixote. They are stories told by other characters. Some of these tales are very long and wonderful.

The parts that I've included are my favorite parts, and the parts I think you'll like the best. Maybe I've embellished things a little, here and there.

A final note: In the many years since Cervantes wrote the book, much about the world has changed and much has not.

Human nature doesn't seem to move along. If you read the newspapers, you'll know that people can be intolerant and cruel. And you'll know that this is nothing new.

In Spain, four hundred years ago, it was against the law to be a Muslim or a Jew. The Muslims in this book are Moors. You'll see them sometimes cast here as the villains. Did Cervantes really think of Moors as villains? I doubt it. But he was writing in a time and place in which an era of some openness to difference had given way to forces of repression. So goes the world, back and forth.

Finally another thing about our world that hasn't changed: there are lots of people in the world who need to feel their lives must mean more than they seem to as they proceed from day to day to day to day to day. These people have a kind of hope and longing. These are things they share with Don Quixote.

But now, we'll travel back in time – four centuries – to meet that famous figure Don Quixote and set out with him on the roads of Spain.

God speed to you, dear Reader, and not just through the pages of this book.

THE FIRST PART

THE COUNTRY GENTLEMAN
BECOMES DON QUIXOTE

戡戡戡

There was a man who lived in a small village in La Mancha, in Spain. For that time, for that place, he was an ordinary man.

The hero of this book had no great wealth. He was an *hidalgo*, which means he was a gentleman but nothing very grand. On the social ladder he was only high enough that working for a living would have been beneath his station. He was not so far up the rungs to properly be called a "Don." You'll soon hear how he came upon this title.

He had money just enough to provide him with a pigeon for his supper once a week, eggs to eat on Saturdays, and meat stews on most days for lunch. Our hero lived this way for many days, for many weeks, for many months, for many years.

He had two sets of clothes – one for everyday and one for special occasions. He had a hired boy to serve him, and a housekeeper. He had a horse – an old one – and a dog for racing. Also living with him was his niece, and she was roughly twenty years of age.

When this tale begins, the man was fifty. His face had caved in from the years.

This was Don Quixote.

The book reports his brain dried up from reading. He stayed up in his room, reading night and day. He had sold off land to buy more books.

He only read one sort of book – tales of chivalry that many people loved to read. They were stories of a made-up past – a past full of adventure and enchantment. It was a world of wizards, of dwarves and giants, monsters, damsels in distress, and kings and queens and dragons. The stories told of magic lakes and palaces, of battles and great time-less loves, and deaths escaped by fractions of an inch.

The heroes of these books were called "knights-errant," and they were men who walked the Earth to right its wrongs. Their mission was to help the needy and comfort the weak. These knights were pure of heart and brave and skilled in battle. They would end up as legends. Time would not erase that they had lived here on this Earth. They'd leave behind much more than well-thumbed books and pigeon bones and pots that once held weekday stews.

Sometimes Don Quixote's housekeeper would pass outside his door and hear her master rushing back and forth. In his chambers, Don Quixote's heart was filling up with something new.

Don Quixote was not our character's real name. We don't know what his real name was. Maybe it was Quixada. In Spanish this means jawbone. Maybe it was Quexana, which means cheesecake. It really doesn't matter. Don Quixote de la Mancha is a name that he invented for himself. He thought it sounded like a name a knight might have.

Our character, you see, at this moment of his life – when he had started thinking up new names to call himself – had ceased to see the world as others saw it. He had come to think the tales of chivalry were true. He had started to believe he was a knight. He was living in the books of chivalry, and he'd begun to make a plan to venture forth.

First off, he had some practical concerns. Quixote would need armor. He had some, left to him by family. He polished up his armor and felt that it would do. And he would need a helmet. He had a sort of helmet – another relic ancestors had left behind. The helmet had no visor and no safeguard for the face.

He made a visor using molded paper. He tested it – he hit it with his sword. It fell apart. And so Quixote made another visor. This time he knew enough to be more careful. He didn't test the visor – not this time. This time he just decided it would do.

The knight would need a horse – a fine and dancing steed. Don Quixote had a horse, but his horse was old and thin, with hooves all cracked, with joints and bones that showed up through his hide. He was what they called in Spanish a *rocine* – a nag. Quixote decided to decide that his *rocine* was sprightly. He named him Rocinante, which means that he "was once a nag." No longer.

And there was something else a knight required. Don Quixote had to have a lady fair – a lady he could worship, in whose name he could do great things. This was a necessity for knights. It gave these men a reason to be great.

The lady must be beautiful, best she should be clever, possibly the daughter of a king and queen, and chaste – untouched by men.

Now, ladies fair in La Mancha, as in every other place, are scarce. And complicating matters even more was this: Don Quixote was not at all in love. But Quixote would be practical in this as well. He settled on a girl he'd once admired from afar. He'd never had the courage to approach her. He had laid eyes on her only four times, but this was no impediment. She didn't need to know she was his lady fair. She didn't need to know that he existed, as likely she did not.

This girl whom he had chosen was a peasant, not a princess – adjustments of imagination were required. But Quixote's ingenuity was equal to the task. He decided to decide that she was fitting as a lady fair. She was reborn. He named her Dulcinea del Toboso.

Was she beautiful and clever? Was she refined? And was she chaste? Let's not waste time on details. Any moment we will leave La Mancha.

渲

One morning, Don Quixote climbed into his armor, fastened on his visor with green ribbons, and climbed upon his steed. He fixed his thoughts upon his lady fair and – saying nothing to his housekeeper and niece, in dark of night – set off.

He was very tall and thin – too thin. If you'd seen him it's the first thing you would have noticed. He was carrying a lance or sword and shield.

In his mind's eye, did he cut a handsome figure? Was he like the characters in books, high up on his horse?

How can we know how Don Quixote saw things? Did he really think he was a knight? We readers must feel free to disagree. But Don Quixote's thoughts can never hide from us his clatter and decrepitude and age – how little like a hero from the storybooks he seemed. They do not hide from us that his visor was made out of molded paper, and the ways that Rocinante was nothing like the charging steeds that thunder through the books of chivalry.

He made his way along the roads away from home. The dawn rose up around him. He let his Rocinante choose the route. Knights do this sometimes in books, to let adventures find them as they would.

DON QUIXOTE BECOMES A KNIGHT

⌒ΠΠΟ

I t was the hottest of hot days. The sun came up and
pelted heat down on the dusty road. Hotter. Hotter.
Not a day to ride in armor, behind a heavy paper
mask, holding up a heavy wooden shield.

But Don Quixote didn't pay attention to his sweating
and discomfort and the dust. Knights would never dwell
on low concerns like these. Furthermore, he had a pressing
matter to attend to, for nagging at our valiant friend was
this: he was not yet officially a knight. Before he could right
wrongs and comfort the needy, there were formalities that
had to be got out of the way.

He and Rocinante traveled on all day and finally – as
much as Don Quixote knew himself not to be slave to
bodily concerns – he and his horse grew tired. They, man
and beast, grew hungry as the sky began to dim.

Where would they spend the night? What would they find for dinner? Somehow, as if by magic, a castle came into view. It rose and shimmered in the air. Atop the castle were four gleaming towers. Around it lay a moat. Across the moat there stretched a drawbridge and past the bridge, the castle's splendid gates.

Don Quixote heard the blastings of a horn. He knew just what this was: the castle dwarf announcing the arrival of a guest.

In just the sort of scene that he'd imagined in his quiet rooms, two enchanting maidens were taking in the air beside the gates. Quixote made his way across the bridge.

"Your ladyships need not flee," said he, "nor fear any rudeness. For it would not befit a knight such as I am to harm a soul, much less such ladies of high station as yourselves."

They found his speech perplexing. He spoke just like a character from books. And as to his appearance: tall and thin, on a broken moldy steed, sunburned, dirty, his face concealed behind a slipshod paper mask.

The maidens stopped and stared at Don Quixote, their faces bent in puzzlement. He seemed to them extravagantly strange. But these were damsels who enjoyed a joke. The two began to giggle in their nervousness, and then to laugh out loud.

Now, having looked upon this scene with Don Quixote's eyes, we'll step aside and see it with our own.

This castle was no castle. The castle was an inn – a place where weary travelers would spend the night. These ladies were not maidens. What shall I say? These were women who were hired by the night by travelers – and not the weary kind – eager for a little female company along the way.

Furthermore, there was no castle dwarf. It was the horn of an approaching pig herder that Quixote'd heard as he came near the inn – a pig herder encouraging his pigs to move along.

And coming out the door to greet the guest there was an innkeeper: a fat and pleasant man whom Don Quixote took to be the castle keeper.

The innkeeper took in the sight before him, heard Quixote's greetings, and quickly guessed his visitor was mad. He'd seen all kinds. Good soul he was, and eager for a little fun perhaps, the innkeeper decided he would play along. He welcomed Don Quixote as a knight and, as our hero'd had his feathers ruffled, asked that he forgive the laughing ladies.

Once inside the inn, the ladies – trollops is what ladies in that line of work were called – helped our hero to take off his armor. He'd tied his visor on his head. It could not be removed.

Dinner was old fish and black and moldy bread, which mercifully the knight mistook for something fine. The trollops fed him dinner through the spaces in his mask. Through a hollow reed they poured his wine into his mouth. Quixote soon forgave the two their jeering.

His stomach filled, attended by these little doves, Don Quixote's thoughts returned to knightly things.

He needed to be dubbed a knight. Ingenious Quixote! Here was a solution close at hand! Who was to say a castle keeper couldn't do the honors in a pinch? Surely there was nothing to forbid it. Don Quixote raised the question with his host and the fat and pleasant innkeeper agreed. First thing in the morning he'd oblige.

Rocinante, fed and watered in his stable, slept a well-earned sleep, but for Quixote there was no time to rest. There was a task he'd read about in books. He must protect his armor through the night. From whom? Well, on to other things.

In the courtyard, Quixote set his armor out against the well. Holding high his lance and shield, his helmet and his visor on his head, wearing only undergarments, Don Quixote marched about within the courtyard walls.

He was tired but would not lay his weary and be-visored head upon a pillow. Duty. Duty. Duty. He would protect his armor through the night.

And then, alas, a figure came into the yard. A mule driver, muleteers they were called, came out to find some water for his animals. Not predicting he'd encounter a character from storybooks, the muleteer went to move the armor from the well.

Well, according to the books of chivalry, no man may tamper with the armor of a knight. In laying hands on Don Quixote's armor – although he was as ignorant of this as you or I would be – the muleteer would offend the very sacred knightly codes. And so he would offend Don Quixote. And thereby he'd insult the Lady Dulcinea too. This our noble friend would not abide.

Quixote's eyes began to stare, his fists to clench, his teeth to grind and creak. And now we'll see a remedy to which Don Quixote would endlessly, wholeheartedly, and eagerly resort.

Casting eyes to heaven, Don Quixote said these words: "Oh, aid me, my Lady Dulcinea. Keep me in your favor and protection." He rushed to where the muleteer stood, raised his lance, and smashed the poor bewildered man upon the head.

As Don Quixote's victim dropped unconscious to the ground, another muleteer came into the yard. Like the first, he only wanted water for his mules. He crossed the yard to move Quixote's armor.

Don Quixote didn't take the time to send up further supplications to his lady. He hurried to the object of his wrath. He raised his lance and brought it down so hard upon his foe, he broke his quarry's head into four parts.

Victory was his! But victory would not be his to savor.

At the noises coming from the yard – at the clanking and the clumping and the gasps and supplications – the mule drivers' companions came running and were, of course, aghast at what they found. They picked up stones and hurled them at Quixote who, being only one thin knight assailed by burly muleteers, fell beneath the rain of rocks.

He squalled with anger as he sank and faltered. "Base and vile rabble," he called out. They would be punished for their onslaught on a great knight such as he!

That first night might have been the end of Don Quixote, but luck was on our hero's side. The fat and friendly innkeeper heard his storm of curses. He came into the courtyard and he stayed the mob. The crowd picked up the wounded muleteers and bore them off.

It was later on, by light of moon, once he'd found the strength to rise and stand that Don Quixote finally became a knight. He was dubbed so by the innkeeper – by the power that is vested in hoteliers – by the touch of his own lance, and witnessed by the damsels who earned money by the hour.

Don Quixote Rescues a Boy;
A Fight in Dulcinea's Name;
The First Sally Ends

In calmer moments at the inn – before the armor and the muleteers and the pelting of the rocks – the innkeeper had offered Don Quixote some advice.

Learning that Quixote had no money, and thus no plans to pay his room and board, he told the knight that knights should bring provisions.

The innkeeper said this: "Of course in books they don't have time to go into the details of supplies. The books insist on focusing on adventures and romance. Still, a knight must be prepared. You must have money. You will need extra shirts and bandages, and magic healing balm will come in handy. You will need it to be healed after a battle, unless you have a magic sage along to cure you, or reason to believe you will be rescued from your trials by a maiden flying in on clouds, or dwarves.

"But most of all, each knight should have a squire at his side. A knight needs a companion, a man to serve and aid in his pursuits."

Despite the furor and the fighting in the courtyard, Don Quixote remembered what the innkeeper had said. By morning, our great knight had made new plans. He would go home and would equip himself with knightly things: a little cash, some shirts, a squire. Perhaps some magic balm.

And so the next day early, the knight set off. Rocinante on that morning was as fleet and nimble as an elderly, decrepit nag can be. Horses know when they are going home.

They set out from the inn, the two of them – limping, creaking merrily along. But fate was to delay them on their way. From somewhere in the trees they heard a cry.

What luck! thought Don Quixote. *Someone in distress!* His services were called upon so soon!

Did Rocinante sigh and roll his eyes? Perhaps. Don Quixote pulled the reins and changed their course and rode into the wood.

And what a sight they found! A boy tied to a tree. He was perhaps fifteen. Poor child! A farmer had a belt raised up to strike him. The farmer struck. The boy cried out again.

If ever there were weak to rescue, then this was he. Here was needy to be comforted! This clearly was a situation calling for a knight. Quixote rode to the awful scene and demanded that the farmer stop his arm.

"Sir Knight," the farmer answered meekly, for Quixote'd caught him quite off guard, "this boy has earned his punishment. He's entrusted to watch over my flock of sheep but so careless that he loses one each day. To punish him, I take the value of the sheep from what he's owed, but he insists I do so out of meanness. Not only is he careless, but he lies."

Quixote, judge and jury, acted quickly. The boy was right, he said, the farmer wrong.

"By the sun that shines above," he thundered at the farmer, "I have half a mind to run thee through."

To run him through? To kill him? To kill the man for hitting this young shepherd with his belt? How Quixote had determined that the boy was blameless we don't know. Perhaps it was Quixote's appetite to right a wrong. But brandishing his lance, Quixote forced the farmer to untie the boy.

"And pay him," warned the knight, "or I'll return and hunt you out and punish you, though you might skulk about and hide and cower like a lizard." Quixote, task behind him, spurred his horse and jingled off toward the road.

Once the knight was gone, the farmer caught the boy again. Before Quixote'd intervened, the farmer's whipping was to mete out punishment. Now he had humiliation to avenge as well. The boy paid dearly for Quixote's help.

But onward! We must not wring our hands at minor points. For more awaits us on the road to home.

⟋⟋⟍⟍⟍⟍⟍⟍

For what was now to come, I think we can give credit to our hero's love of Lady Dulcinea. Otherwise it makes no sense at all.

Six merchants and their party came toward the knight and squire on the road. They were traveling from town to town, carrying the silk they had to sell. Six merchants holding sunshades, four servants on their horses, three boys on foot with loaded mules in tow. For them this was a normal day of work.

But did Don Quixote see before him only merchants? He did not. What he saw before him were knights-errant. It seems that they were not the sort he liked.

Quixote stopped his horse to block their path. He held his lance up high, the way he'd read that knights of old would do, and called out in a booming knightly voice, "All of you stop! Unless you will confess that in the world there is no maiden fairer than the Empress of La Mancha, the matchless and perfect Dulcinea del Toboso."

The silk merchants, as you might guess, had never heard of Dulcinea, as indeed the girl did not exist. Nor had they, it's safe to say, been stopped before to answer questions such as this, posed by men in threadbare fancy dress.

However uninformed the merchants were about the lovely Lady Dulcinea, one thing they knew full well. This fellow who had stopped their little caravan had lost his wits. Perhaps he could provide a little fun.

One of the six spoke up. He was a fellow known for pranks and humor.

"Sir Knight, we do not know who this good lady is. If she be the beauty you suggest, of course, we will agree to what you're asking. Perhaps there is a chance that we could see her?"

"How dare you!" said Quixote. "The point is this: you must believe, confess, affirm, and swear she is the loveliest. I hope you are not telling me that you require proof?"

"Sir Knight," the fellow spoke again, "perhaps you have upon you some small portrait. A likeness that's no bigger than a grain of wheat would do. Otherwise, how could we know," he asked, "that she is not, for instance, blind in one eye and maybe leaking fluids from the other?"

Well, you can picture Don Quixote's anger. "She is not one-eyed," he bellowed. "There are no fluids running from the other! Nor is she a hunchback!" He added this. And how can we know why?

Don Quixote kicked his horse to charge. But Rocinante must have had his mind on other things. Perhaps the horse was taken by surprise. In any case, he did not charge. Instead of lunging forward into battle, he tripped and toppled over, tossing Don Quixote to the ground.

And there he lay, Quixote, tangled in his armor, flapping like a wounded bird, spitting threats and insults, until another of the group grew tired of his noisy helpless tantrum.

A merchant grabbed Quixote's lance and broke it into pieces, and beat him with the bits of shattered sticks. Quixote, persisting in his insults, only made his punishment grow worse and worse. And worse.

Soundly, sorely thrashed, Quixote lay upon the ground. The merchants, returning to the business of their day, made off.

Our hero was so badly bruised he found that he could not regain his feet and so he took advantage of the chance that his infirmity provided to consider what at first had seemed to be defeat. At first. On reflection, things had turned out rather well.

He must keep in mind, he mused, that this was Rocinante's fault and not his own. A world of difference. He lay there with a fine view of the sky. He realized, what's more, that this adventure was the sort of thing a real-life knight would have. This had been a battle for the honor of his lady. He was indeed a knight at last, and doing knightly things!

He lay there on the dusty road – victorious, if not equipped to stand. Rocinante, most obliging when it came to standing still, stayed close.

The day wore on. The sun beat down.

Finally, it seems Quixote's dried-out brain had dried out even further. He slipped free of the bonds of his invented self.

But he did not become the gentleman who had two sets of clothes and pigeon for his dinner once a week. He now turned into other knights – other knights he'd read about in books. He lay there mumbling the passages he'd heard these other heroes speak and mixed in famous verses of the sort that Spanish children learn at school.

At last a local farmer, passing by, came upon our hero on the ground. A kind and friendly fellow, he crouched down to Quixote. He recognized the knight.

"Señor Quixada?" asked the farmer. "What has brought you to this pass?"

To which our hero answered, "Where are you, lady mine? Do you not feel sorrow at my suffering? You can not know what I endure, or else you do not love me!"

In other words, Don Quixote made no hint of sense at all.

The farmer draped our friend across his donkey's back. He took up Rocinante's reins and, leading him, set off for home.

At the outskirts of Quixote's town, the farmer waited until dark to bring the beaten would-be knight into the village. He did this to conceal Quixote's sad condition – a quiet act of kindness by a stranger, giving comfort to a needy knight.

Don Quixote's Books Are Burned; He Recruits the Peasant Sancho Panza; The Second Sally Begins

Three days had passed since Don Quixote'd left his home. Frantic were his housekeeper and niece. Frantic were his friends, the barber and the priest. For three long days, the four had fumed and wrung their hands. They heated up the little house with worry.

His frenzied niece retold the story of the days before her uncle had escaped. He had told her he'd been battling with giants and that the sweat that blossomed on his face was blood. He'd told her that his water jug was filled with magic potions. It was the books he read that drove him mad.

As the farmer bearing Don Quixote came near the house, he heard the anxious rantings from within. *This poor old man*, the farmer thought, *he thinks he is a hero from a book!* Respecting the delusions of his passenger, he called out that he'd brought a wounded knight.

And so Quixote was brought home. Battered and bewildered though he was, the *hidalgo* who'd gone missing was alive. But he was, they soon discovered, still a knight.

"Stop," Quixote said, addressing those who loved him, those who crowded close with smiles and falling tears. "Stop. I am wounded. I am wounded through my horse's fault."

They took the knight to bed. Before Quixote slept, he told the group that he'd been crushed by giants. Ten giants. Giants that were terrible and huge.

He'd been crushed by giants? And this was somehow Rocinante's fault? We don't have time to dwell on points of logic.

The great knight Don Quixote fell asleep.

⁊⁊⁊

Morning came. Quixote slept. But from the break of day the household, all about him, was abuzz.

The barber and the priest arrived. With the ladies of the house, they planned to take to task those blackguards who'd brought on the derangement of their friend – the books.

"There is no reason," said the niece, "for showing any mercy to these scoundrels."

Planning their campaign, the foursome climbed the stairs to where the villains lurked upon the shelves. Perhaps a hundred books awaited trial: handsome, leather-bound – rascals in such opulent disguise.

The barber took them off the shelves one by one and gave them to the priest to pass his sentence. And wonderfully convenient, the priest was quite familiar with their contents.

Once condemned, the books were given over to the ladies, the appointed executioners. At their hands the books would die by fire.

One book was doomed and then another. And then, perhaps, a title would be spared.

The ladies didn't waste their precious time in running up and down the stairs. Out the window went the books, to spend their final hours in an ever-growing pile in the yard.

Another book was for the fire and then another.

And then sometimes a book was set aside. Here was a book they need not burn; perhaps it could be hidden down a well. Of another book, the priest decreed: "This devil we will lock up instead of burning. We'll build a little coffin for a cell." And of another book the priest would spare, "This one we will forgive, as it was written by a king."

And then another to the flames. And then another.

"And here's one we must rescue, to be certain! This book is by the author named Cervantes!"

On the days of the great purge, Don Quixote rose from bed just once. The foursome heard him shouting in his room. They found him up and stabbing at his enemies, striking at the walls. They calmed him down and put him back to bed.

Finally, in the library, the crusaders finished off their task and shut the door. They shut the door and nailed it shut and walled it off and papered over where the door had been. The door was gone. The room was gone. The books – or most of them – had perished in the courtyard in the fire.

When Don Quixote finally awoke, his housekeeper explained his books were gone. An enchanter took the books, she said. He rode in on a serpent, did his evil dealings in the library, and disappeared by flying through the roof.

When he rose from bed, Quixote was every bit as much a knight as ever. He did not doubt his housekeeper's account. Enchanters would select him as a target. He was such a great knight, after all.

⌘

Though outwardly he seemed to have put aside his plans for more adventures, Don Quixote went about collecting his supplies.

He sold some goods and pawned some goods and thereby laid his hands upon the money he would need to take along. He fixed his broken helmet and his visor and packed some extra shirts. He had no magic potion – not just yet.

But of all the things he gathered to go back into the world, the knight's most crucial item was his squire.

What we know of Sancho Panza when we meet him is only that he was a local peasant – a simple farmer with a wife and children. He was fat – we know this too, for *Panza* is a Spanish word for belly.

And Sancho was not what one might consider clever. So little wit he had, it seems, that he believed the promises that Don Quixote made.

Don Quixote told his squire – and certainly believed it to be true – that the squire of a knight could reasonably expect some lofty post as a reward: this would be the payment for his service. Chances were that he'd be made a governor. Maybe he'd become an earl. The ruler of an island. Or a king.

Furthermore, this might not take too long. In books, the squires had to wait until old age to reap their prize. Quixote planned to do the books one better. He thought that Sancho Panza should be prepared that all of this might happen in a week!

Sancho brought his donkey, a beast he dearly loved. Sancho filled and brought along his saddlebags and wineskins. He stuffed his bags with food and drink. No extra shirts for him. He packed to meet the dictates of his stomach.

The two told no one of their plan. They met in secret so that they would not be followed, and made off in the night.

In the darkness we can barely see them: a tall thin man in armor on a weary, skinny mount and a short man on an ass with saddlebags.

The night wore on. They made their way along the Spanish roads away from home.

What was Sancho thinking as they set off on their journey? That he would be a governor or king? Did he marvel at the turn his life had taken? Did he think of his good fortune? Or of the many risks he might be taking? Sancho raised just one concern with Don Quixote, a worry that involved the squire's wife.

He told the knight that his wife was very simple. God bless her, she was just the sort of wife a simple fellow like a peasant farmer wants. The trouble was, the squire said, she might not be quite fitting for a gentleman of higher rank, such as Sancho Panza would become. Now, this was meant as no insult to her, but, frankly, she wouldn't do to be the consort of a governor or king. To tell the truth, she wasn't even good enough for countess.

Quixote mulled this over. Whatever were her failings, he pronounced, they must not keep the squire from his destiny. God would find some proper fate for Sancho Panza's wife.

This resolved, the two men traveled on – off into the world and on their way. No housekeepers, no nieces, and no wives.

Don Quixote Fights with Windmills

⁂

Whatever occupied the thoughts of these two men – once they had discussed the trifling destinies of wives – these thoughts would now be put aside.

The sun rose up and spread across the sky. Ahead there stretched a field. And in the field appeared, to Don Quixote's startled eyes, a crowd of men.

But these were men too massive to be men of any normal kind. What stood ahead were giants, so tall their arms were fully six miles long. They stood a crowd of thirty, maybe more, and all of them, as one, regarded Don Quixote and his squire, looking down from far up in the heavens, heavens that they blackened with their mighty forms.

They lifted up and swung their arms, their fists rose up and dropped, flew to the skies, and dropped to Earth – whistling, heavy through the air.

And it would be Quixote's task to put these thirty giants to their death. It was God's work, he told the squire. "Giants, when encountered, should be taken from the Earth."

It's surprising that Quixote even heard his squire's answer, with the passions churning in his head, with all the frenzy firing his bony breast.

As Don Quixote spurred on Rocinante, Sancho Panza raised his voice. The question Don Quixote likely did not hear was this: "What giants?" Sancho cried. "What looms ahead are windmills!"

Windmills. The word rang out behind Quixote's charging horse.

"Fly not, you cowards and vile beings," Quixote shouted to the giants in his path. "A single knight advances to attack you."

The giants did not flee. The thirty massive monsters held their ground.

Quixote hurtled forward with his lance aloft. He charged – this skinny clanking figure (wrongheaded, brave), this rickety misguided hero on his rusty mount. He charged and drove his lance into his nearest foe.

The weapon met its mark. But it was not a giant's swinging arm it pierced. It was a sail – a windmill's sail – which caught the lance and lifted up the horse and rider. It sent them flying through the air, and then it threw them crashing to the ground. It was indeed as if Quixote had been lifted up and tossed aside by giants. It's dangerous, as well, to charge at windmills.

Sancho Panza made his way to where his master lay, crumpled and discarded by the windmill's arm, Rocinante thrown beside him in the dust.

"I told you they were windmills." said the squire.

But if the knight's spare frame was bruised and broken, his ingenuity was not at all impaired.

"These are windmills now," Quixote said. "They became so in the instant that my lance approached. What has happened is the work of a magician – perhaps the very one who stole my books! He has done this thing to rob me, to steal from me the joy of killing giants."

This reasoning now spoken – Sancho Panza's error now set straight – Quixote had his duties to attend to.

He rose up to his knees and to his feet. It wouldn't be his way, if he could help it, to loll about, to dwell on battles now behind him. Not when there were so many wrongs that needed righting in the world and needy to be comforted and chores to do.

First off, he must replace his lance. He knew from books he'd need a bough of oak.

Rocinante's shoulder was quite battered. It had been wrestled (by the giant) from its socket. Time would cure the horse. For now, he must regain his hooves.

And on they went. Don Quixote chose a road he knew to be well traveled – the sort of road that promised them adventure.

The Princess in the Coach

⟡

A head of us, dear reader, is a story with a crack right down the middle – like a picture that's been torn in half and then has been repaired and patched together.

⟡

Our friends the knight and squire hobbled down the road toward adventure.

Don Quixote, as you know, was injured, tilting over on his injured horse. This was the price he paid for fighting windmills. Sancho, on the other hand, found the windmill fight had put wind in his sails. For him there had been no harm done. This wasn't very difficult, the work of squires. Or so he thought that day.

Sancho Panza opened up his saddlebags and wineskin. He ate and drank atop his ambling ass. A man like Sancho needed more than food for thought and luckily, he'd brought a lot along.

But true to form, Don Quixote fixed his thoughts on loftier concerns than lunch. Knights did not give in to thirst or hunger, nor did they obey their aches and pains.

"A knight does not complain of injuries. Even if his guts were ripped wide open," he said. "Even if his bowels were torn and spilling out upon the ground. Perhaps he'd grit his teeth. It's possible some hint of pain would cross his handsome face. He would not moan and groan. He would not carry on as others might."

Sancho chewed his lunch and listened.

"A knight such as I may not complain. But I think you'll be glad to hear, these standards do not apply to squires."

When darkness came they found a spot to stop. Quixote found a bough of oak to make a lance.

That night, Quixote did not eat. He did not sleep. He had no time to rest. He knew there was a duty he'd neglected. For knights there is so very much to do. He had not spent sufficient time in longing. By dark of night, as Sancho slept, Don Quixote spent the hours longing for his Lady Dulcinea.

⁂

The story with the crack that's been repaired is now upon us, and starts up the middle of the afternoon to come.

Somehow Don Quixote sensed events approaching. He stopped his horse and looked about and said to Sancho Panza, "Here we'll plunge our arms into adventure."

On the road a group of travelers approached.

Two friars in black robes rode in front on mules as tall as camels. Their faces were concealed by masks to protect them from the sun and dirt.

With these two men on mules there were two mule-teers. Behind them there was a coach. Inside the coach sat a lady and with her rode her servants.

The lady in the coach was on her way to meet her husband at the coast. From there the two would leave for the Americas. Her husband was to take up some new post.

Such were the facts, but this was not the way things looked to Don Quixote. He saw instead a pair of bad magicians or enchanters accompanied by evil magic helpers. This scurvy group was kidnapping a princess!

So Don Quixote undertook his duty. Despite the warnings of his squire, who saw the friars for the men of God they were, Don Quixote stopped the men atop tall mules.

"Devilish and unnatural beings," said Quixote, "release the highborn princess you have stolen. Or else prepare to meet a speedy death!"

The friars stopped their mules. Astonished as they were, they gave an answer: "We are not devilish or unnatural," said one. "We do not know if there is a captive princess in the coach behind us."

This was just the sort of lie magicians and enchanters like to tell. Perhaps they took Quixote for a fool! How dare they? How dare they pay this insult to a knight!

"I know you! Lying rabble!" said Quixote. "No soft words with me!" He raised his lance and charged into the closest of the two.

The friar who was charged fell from his horse. The other – shocked and terrified – spurred his mule and rode away. He would watch the outcome from a distance.

Thus Quixote dealt with the enchanters. How baffling this must have been, even for men as used to mystery as men of God.

If Sancho Panza was not informed of all the finer points of chivalry, at least he seemed to know his rights as squire. The belongings of a beaten foe were his. So Sancho Panza descended on the fallen friar, tore off the friar's flowing robes and, moving over to the mule, stripped the beast of all he held as well.

How very sad for Sancho that the fallen friars' muleteers did not have even Sancho's scanty grasp of knightly code. They turned on the squire as though he were a common thief. They threw our Sancho Panza to the ground and thrashed and whipped and kicked him. They pulled out every hair from off his chin!

Sancho conquered thus, the muleteers raised the fallen friar to his feet, placed him on his mule, and led him off.

Meanwhile Don Quixote, still atop his horse, ventured to the coach to reap his thanks.

"My beauteous lady," said Quixote, leaning in the window of the lady's coach, "for my brave service, I ask that you return to El Toboso. Present yourself before the Lady Dulcinea and tell her what I have done to set you free."

Well, we will never know what Quixote's rescued princess might have found to answer to the narrow paper-covered face that loomed into the window of her coach. For one of her attendants, the antics of our hero had grown stale. He yelled, "Be gone!" He grabbed Quixote's lance and demanded that Quixote let them pass.

Ingratitude! Ingratitude and disrespect! The knight must answer with his famous arm!

Don Quixote unsheathed his dreadful sword. He would teach this hooligan a lesson. But the ingrate did not flinch. He shared Quixote's willingness to fight. He had a sword as well. He brought it out and struck Quixote with such force that, had Quixote not had on his armor, the sword blow would have split him down the middle.

Quixote raised his sword above his head. His fury found each drop of strength within him. He held his lance above his head to swing. Rage can make the frailest of us strongmen. In his bones Quixote knew, as strangely did they all, that he would summon up a strike so violent this enemy might die right then and there.

A hush.

Fear pooled in the bowels of the lady's squire. He had no shield. He snatched a little pillow from inside the coach. With nothing but the pillow to protect him, he froze in place to await Quixote's blow. He raised his sword as well.

And so stood Don Quixote with his sword aloft, with murder in his heart, strength in his arm. His adversary waited, protected from his foe by just a pillow. Make no mistake; his arm was strong as well. Just now he had dealt the knight a blow that might have killed him.

All around them stared with horror at the scene, dreading what was to come. This would end in grief and gore.

And this is where the story breaks in half.

THE SECOND PART

THE CRACK IN THE STORY

As you know, Cervantes pretends that he didn't write the story he is telling. He tells us that he only found a part of it at first – the part that ends with Don Quixote and the lady's squire with their swords aloft.

But he had faith that the story of so great a knight would somewhere have been told in full.

Was he right? And where on earth? Would the story fall into Cervantes' hands? Two cliffhangers at once.

And then, one day at the market in Toledo, Cervantes writes that he came upon a boy who sold old notebooks. The notebooks were in Arabic, a language that Cervantes did not know. To find out what the notebooks had to say, he found a fellow to translate the pages.

How astonishing is chance! Here it was! He'd found more of the story of Quixote, written by an historian – a Moor.

Do you find the matter of the authorship confusing? Does your head begin to spin? Is it hard to know for certain who is who and what is what?

Let me assure you, Mr. Cervantes does not mind.
He returns us to the road in Spain.
Don Quixote's holding up his sword. The lady's squire is
shielded by the pillow.

The Battle Is Resolved; An Evening Among Goatherds; Grisóstomo

It was the lady's squire and not Quixote who struck first. He struck the knight so powerful a blow it cut Quixote's helmet in two and chopped off half his ear. Quixote's armor shattered into pieces and scattered all about him on the ground.

But in landing such a gruesome blow, the lady's squire found a way to lose the fight. The indignity of injury made Quixote's breast explode with rage. Made powerful by anger, Quixote, rising in his stirrups, raised his sword and, even through the cushion, landed such a clout upon the squire that the man began to spout his blood through eyes and nose and ears and mouth.

The bloodied squire's mule shied back and spun about to run. The lady's squire, awash in gore, slithered from his mount down to the ground.

Quixote pressed his victory. Jumping, clanking from his horse, Quixote stood above his glistening prey and placed his sword between the man's two eyes.

The lady in the coach called out, begging for her squire to be spared.

Don Quixote put his sword away. He'd spare the man, but under one condition. The bloodied squire must go to El Toboso, present himself to Lady Dulcinea and tell her Don Quixote de la Mancha had fought evil magicians in her name.

The lady and her squire, of course, agreed.

As these tumultuous events took place, Sancho Panza lay upon the ground listening as his master waged the battle for his life. He listened but his mind was somewhere else: would this adventure bring him his reward?

⟨⟩

After Don Quixote's fight was done – once the other characters had gathered up their wits and their belongings and gone away – Sancho Panza helped his master to remount his weary horse and raised the nagging matter of reward.

"May it please your worship," asked the squire, "to give me whatever island we have won in this hard fight?"

"Not now," said Don Quixote. "This is not the sort of fight that gives us islands. This is merely an encounter at a crossroads, in which we will gain nothing but a broken head."

But Sancho Panza must not be discouraged, said the knight who was in good cheer despite his wounds. As the pair rode off, Don Quixote – conqueror, rescuer of princesses – took the time to fill his squire in on other facets of the knightly life.

So much to learn.

For instance: Don Quixote's newly butchered ear. This wound could easily be cured, he said, if only he had brought along some healing balm of Fierabras. It was a mixture mentioned in a famous Spanish tale.

To describe its magic power, Don Quixote told his squire this: if (for example) he, Quixote, were somehow cut in half – and this occurred more often than you'd think – Sancho could simply fit the pieces of his master back together, take the half that lay upon the ground, and place it fast against the half that still sat upright in the saddle. This must be done before the blood congeals. Then he should serve the knight two mouthfuls of the balm. If the squire had the pieces matching up just right, Quixote would be cured.

"For all these tasks," said Sancho, not savoring the prospect of clotting blood and cloven knights, "at least I can console myself that I will soon be ruler of an island."

"You should consider carefully," his master answered. "You might prefer to rule some landlocked place. Perhaps you'd like to be the King of Denmark."

Quixote asked the squire if there might be a little food left over in his bag. Knights would often go without for weeks on end eating nothing but the flowers of the field. But just this once he was a little peckish.

⁂

Whatever were the contents of the saddlebags, the problem of their dinner was soon solved. No castle rose up in the road before them. Instead they found a campfire and some goatherds. There were six of them – generous and kindly souls.

They gave the knight a seat before the fire. They offered up a hearty stew, chunks of meat as big as fists, acorns, and a wheel of aging cheese. The wineskin passed from hand to hand to hand.

The wineskin is the keeper of a thousand moods. Love, at times. Nostalgia or violence or peevishness perhaps. From in its folds emerge, depending on the time and place and customer, resentments, sometimes merriment, high spirits and low, and sweet contentment.

On this night, the wineskin had the latter to provide to Don Quixote. Heart warmed and stomach filled, the knight became most splendidly contented and found he had some wisdom to impart.

To the dozing wine-soaked goatherds, Don Quixote delivered forth the thoughts that their good will had conjured up. Their kindness recalled to him just how life used to be, he said. There was a time he called "the golden age."

"Happy was the age, happy the time," began Quixote, "which was called the golden age. In those days things were never known by names like 'thine' or 'mine.' All things were shared. And all that was required for daily food was to reach and take the acorns from the trees. The streams and running brooks gave us their water. The bees offered their honey to be taken. The mighty cork trees gave their bark for shelter.

"All was peace and friendship. Shepherdesses, innocent and beautiful, could wander as they wished, unmolested, wearing only leaves. Truth reigned and with it ruled sincerity. Justice held. Laws had not been written. None were needed. It is to bring this era back," he told the woozy goatherds, "that knights like I – Quixote – walk this Earth."

He waxed on as the goatherds, no doubt, waned. In the dark a young man sang a song and played the fiddle.

A goatherd made a paste of rosemary and salt. He chewed it and pressed it onto Don Quixote's tattered ear. He said that it would heal Quixote's wound.

It did.

༄༄༄

But the party would not end just yet. A visitor arrived to join the sodden circle – a visitor who bore a tale of tragic love.

Now, as to love, a brief aside: Don Quixote's lady fair was his invention, even though he had assigned a peasant girl to hold her place. And while there are some drawbacks to a love affair with one whom one's invented, like Dulcinea, this arrangement has its benefits as well. To start with, one can make the course of love run smoothly.

When beloveds *do* exist, many complications can arise, as in the tale our characters would hear before they fell asleep.

The young man who joined the group around the fire had come here for a burial.

The one who would be buried was Grisóstomo – a man. No, more a boy. Too young to die. His father was a wealthy farmer from the mountains, the boy a student – gifted with the art of telling fortunes from the stars. He was handsome. He was jovial. A wonderful companion. Many people loved him. But not the one whom he loved most. Not the beautiful and merciless Marcela.

She was the orphaned daughter of another farmer and, as a child, had come into great wealth. She'd grown up in the household of her uncle and almost from her childhood was famous far and wide for being beautiful.

She was a modest girl by nature, and though she'd been secluded by her uncle, by the time she was old enough to marry, many men had sought her hand merely on the strength of her description.

Marcela, though, was not inclined to marry – not yet. She didn't want the burdens of a wife. And so to put discussions of her marriage to an end, Marcela left her home and took up life among the shepherd girls.

But exile in the distant hills did not provide her the seclusion that she sought. There was nothing to prevent what now ensued: the immigration to these parts of countless lovesick boys.

Before too long the landscape was aswarm with suitors. They dressed as shepherds – disguised as kindred spirits to entice her. The hillsides whispered out their lovelorn sighs.

One boy in rustic garb spent his hours sprawled on the ground, his eyes turned up and fixed upon the heavens. How he languished! How he longed! Another lay awake all night, felled with anguish he did not disguise. One lover wept; a fourth wrote verse. The bark of trees displayed their names, carved and intertwined with hers.

Grisóstomo was of this broken-hearted throng. Or had been. According to the story, he'd stopped loving her and had begun to worship her instead. He'd died of love, perhaps by his own hand.

At the fireside, the teller of this tale fell silent. The story done, all found a place to close their eyes and rest. Quixote's thoughts flew off to Dulcinea. He knew the joys and sufferings, and all the joyful sufferings of love. In his chest there beat a heart well suited to the lavish raptures of a lovelorn grief.

So mused our Don Quixote underneath the twinkling stars.

Sancho Panza pressed himself against his ass for warmth.

The Cold-Hearted Girl

When morning came, mourners for Grisóstomo thronged to the hills. Don Quixote and his squire followed them to where the grave would be.

The mourners came in sheepskins, dyed pitch black, with oleander and cypress in their hair. They came finely dressed with holly staffs in hand and servants in their wake. They brought the coffin to the place Grisóstomo had said he must be buried – the place where he had first seen fair Marcela.

Marcela. His blood was on her hands – so all agreed as with their tears and pick-axes they worked to put their friend below the ground. Marcela, who could have spared this young man's life, but hadn't.

He lay there in his coffin, Grisóstomo – beautiful himself – bedecked with flowers, victim of this cold, death-dealing girl.

The mourners read a poem from the dead man's pen. He had no hope of happiness, he said. Not in this life. Only death could offer him relief.

Displayed around the young man's body were his poems and his letters. His dearest friend, Ambrosio, summed up his fortunes thus: "He loved deeply, but he was hated. He adored, but he was scorned. He wooed a wild beast. He pleaded with a statue. And for reward was given only death."

But then, look up! High above this busy scene, upon the rocks that overlooked the crowd, a shepherdess appeared. Her beauty brought their toils to a halt. It was Marcela.

All silence save the breezes and the birds.

Finally, it was Ambrosio, Grisóstomo's close friend, who raised his voice. "Have you come to gloat?" he called. "Have you come to revel in your handiwork? Are you here to glory at the sight of fallen prey?"

She calmly gave her answer from atop the rocks. "I've come to speak some words of self-defense," she said. "And then to ask that I be left in peace."

The crowd stood silent, listening and maybe just a little bit bewitched.

"I am loved for being beautiful," she said. "Does that mean I must love whomever loves me? Am I obliged to be in love because someone is in love with me? Am I heartless if I do not happen to return this love? Love is, after all, not something one can choose to feel, even if one wishes to."

Birds and wind. No sound came from the crowd.

"And if a man will love me for my beauty – only for my outward shape and form – must I love him too? And is this true no matter his appearance?

"You may love me for my beauty, and would not love me otherwise, but must I love you in return no matter what sort of man you are? And if I don't then I am called cold-hearted. Even cruel.

"If I were not beautiful, would I be right if I were angry at a man who did not love me, whom I loved? Might I call him cruel? Would he be hard-hearted because he does not feel for me the love that I might feel for him?

"And furthermore," she said, this vision on the rocks above their heads, "I did not ask to be born beautiful. I have done nothing to provoke the love of men. I did not wish it."

She wished to live alone up in the hills. She had told this to their ardent friend, Grisóstomo. But he refused to take her at her word. It was his stubbornness that killed him, so she argued, not anything that she had done or said.

"What I want most is freedom," said the girl. "I have no wish to feel constraint. I neither love nor hate. I do not deceive one man nor court another. The conversation of the shepherd girls and the care of animals are my delight. Everything I'll ever want is bounded by these mountains, and if my thoughts should stray, it will be to contemplate the beauty of the sky above our heads."

Marcela turned and made her way into the woods. Don Quixote put his hand upon his sword. No one was to follow her, he said. She was to be esteemed and not reviled.

The mourners dug the grave and lowered their Grisóstomo into the ground. They closed the grave and sealed it with a heavy stone.

Some among the mourners, mesmerized, made off in the direction that the girl had gone. Whatever were their fates, they had been warned.

As the crowd dispersed, Don Quixote told his squire they would stay here in the hills to foil highwaymen. Perhaps they'd give protection to Marcela.

They rode into the forest. They searched for her two hours but did not find her. That lovely girl. A spirit lifted like a song.

THE THIRD PART

Romance for Rocinante;
Calamities at the Inn

❧

Love takes many forms. The word is quite inadequate to gather up the compulsions and affections and attachments that it's used to represent.

Let us take romantic love again. There is Don Quixote's chaste and perfect love for Dulcinea, a perfection made more possible by their not having met. There is Sancho Panza's time-worn love for his good wife – practical and fault-finding and sturdy. And then there is the sort of love that wells up the hearty hearts of muleteers for damsels whom they hire for the night. Perhaps this latter is the love that overcame our Rocinante on this day.

We come upon a field of grazing mares. To you and me a pretty rural scene. To Don Quixote's horse it was a spectacle with powers that would stir the horse's blood – and bring forth springtime to his wintry breast.

Love's mysteries we'll never plumb. We only know that Rocinante, finding up ahead a field so populated to his taste, summoned up a speed of which no one would have ever dreamed him capable. He trotted into their midst at top speed. Reaching his bewitching prey, he leapt upon whichever he could grasp within his hungry hooves.

Sadly, though, springtime had not come upon their ladyships the mares. They had stopped within the verdant field to graze and were more interested in dinner than in dancing. They bucked and kicked and bit their aging suitor. They shrugged and dodged and wrestled him away. Cruel-hearted, marble-hearted beasts. They refused to love him!

And then the men whose mares these were joined in. Twenty brawny men came forth and beat Quixote's horse with sticks.

Quixote rushed to Rocinante to defend him, and so he too was pummeled by the mob. Sancho Panza fared no better, following his master, and the horse, to his defeat.

Don Quixote, Sancho Panza, Rocinante: they ended this sad episode unconscious on the ground. Oblivion for all. Romantic disappointment for the horse.

The angry owners rounded up their mares and went away.

Sancho was the first to swim up from unconsciousness. "Is it possible," he asked the knight, "you have with you the magic healing potion you once told me of?"

Don Quixote, now returning to the light of day as well, had none.

Neither moved, or only moved their lips with which to speak.

Sancho Panza had another thing to ask. "Not knowing much about the lives of knights and squires," he said, "perhaps you'll tell me if this punishment's the sort of thing that squires are expected to get used to?"

Don Quixote did admit that things like this take place from time to time.

And then a pause, and then another question from the squire. "How many days will we wait until we have the strength to stand and walk?"

How should Don Quixote know? The knight lay still. What a time to pester him with questions!

Before their feet agreed to bear their weight, the two talked on. True to form, Quixote used the time to find a way to see their beating in a proper light.

"To start with," said Quixote, "this outcome is my fault. I see now how this might have been avoided. Our mistake," the knight explained, "is that a knight should never fight with rabble. We are beaten because it is your place to fight with lowborn types. Not mine. And more good news," he said. "There is a reason why this beating, which looks so much like defeat, is not. According to the books, if enemies do not use proper weapons and instead use something that they have on hand – say a cobbler strikes a knight with implements for making shoes – then no indignity is suffered by his enemy."

The horses' minders had used their stakes for moving horses as their bludgeons. Because of this, Quixote told the squire, the owners of the mares were not victors. Sensible or not, it was an age-old wrinkle of the code.

Let's hope they found some comfort in this talk, as they passed the hours lying in the field.

By nightfall they were on the road again. Don Quixote, dignity untouched, was slung over the back of Sancho Panza's ass. Sancho said it this way: "like a sack of garbage." And then, as darkness came, they found an inn.

To Don Quixote's eyes it was a castle.

And now, as to the royalty who lived there. There was an innkeeper, his kindly wife, his very pretty daughter, and a servant girl whose name was Maritornes.

Ah Maritornes! Do words exist to bring her charms to life? She had wide jowls. Her head was flat in back. Her nose was short and snubbed. One eye was blind, the other weak and dim. She stood not five feet high from head to toe. Her shoulders, somewhat humped, forced her feeble gaze toward the ground.

But Maritornes, as you'll see, had qualities aplenty to her credit. Among them were the sorts of things that made her dear to muleteers who might spend the night: a gaiety, a gameness, a way of putting modesty aside for pocket change.

The inn was full that night. The only place for Don Quixote and his squire to sleep was in a hayloft. How lucky that these humble quarters seemed to Don Quixote to be princely. The two would share these chambers with a muleteer.

The women patched up Don Quixote's wounds. He told them he'd been injured by a tumble from a rock. It's always a surprise to hear him lie. Perhaps the knight was actually confused. His story had, of course, a little whiff of fantasy about it. But as soon as it was told it was forgotten. It was a long way from the oddest thing about this guest.

Quixote, bandaged head to toe, thanked the ladies in his courtly style. He told them that their efforts were well spent and that they were not squandering their kindness on some ordinary sort. He was a knight.

"He is a knight for now," Sancho chimed in. "Before too long, he will be raised to even greater heights. In his line of work, and mine, we must not wait too long before the fates transform us into mighty rulers. Between us, I might soon become a king. King Sancho."

And so the day had been resolved quite well. But in the darkness, once the lamps were out, Quixote lay awake. His bed was hard and lumpy. His wounds were sore. His pains kept him from sleeping. They used to put it this way: his eyes remained as open as a hare's.

Now, in this state – exhausted yet not sleeping – our knight began to weave a waking dream.

He came up with the notion that the daughter of the king and queen downstairs had no sooner laid eyes on him than she loved him. The princess, whom he'd met only that night, had lost her heart. Poor girl. He could sense, for he was very sensitive, that she was suffering downstairs. It was as though he heard her throbbing heart right through the floor. Lying there the knight began to fret.

Though the love of princesses is flattering to any aging, injured, bandaged knight, her ardor in this instance posed a problem. For surely she would not resist her need to climb the stairs to find him. She was only human after all. In which event, he asked himself, what should he do? He was promised to his lovely lady fair. Poor princess. He knew that he must dash her girlish dreams.

And then, as he'd predicted, a female figure came through the door.

It was Maritornes. Earlier that day she'd met the mule-teer. He had felt the sort of love for darling Maritornes that Rocinante had for grazing mares.

She had arranged to meet him in this room. And Maritornes was a girl who kept her promises – a sterling quality, for sure. The company of unexpected roommates did not make her break her word for she was not encumbered by decorum. And so the muleteer lay awake as well, his eyes as open as a hare's, waiting for her step upon the stair.

The room was dark – too dark to let Quixote see it was the servant girl who had come in. And somehow, passing by his bed, she ended up in Don Quixote's arms. It was the princess, thought Quixote.

Maritornes's dress was made of sackcloth, but beneath his touch Quixote felt fine linen. Maritornes's hair was coarser than a horse's mane. Quixote found upon her head soft threads of gold. Maritornes's breath carried with it stark reminders of a day-old salad. Don Quixote's nose met sweet perfume.

She struggled to be free of him. Quixote, though, would not release his catch. Not before he could explain the reasons that he must resist her invitation. He insisted he explain, in full, at length. His romantic fate, he whispered to the girl, lay somewhere else.

She did her very best to get away. The knight would not let go.

It was finally the muleteer who brought Quixote's endless kind rejections to a close. Once aware the knight had trapped the girl who had been meant for him, he rose up from his bed and crossed the room. He hit Quixote squarely in the jaw.

Suddenly, the mouth that had poured forth such fancy words now poured forth blood. And as the girl escaped, the muleteer jumped upon the injured knight. He leapt upon Quixote on the bed. It was a bed not meant for such gymnastics. The bed collapsed. A crash. And then a cry came up the stairs.

It was the innkeeper, the king! If there was trouble in the night, he knew full well whose name to call. He climbed the stairs bellowing for Maritornes, who, piling one mistake upon another, fled and quite by accident ended up on Sancho Panza's bed.

Woken from his sleep, the squire shrieked and flailed. He was asleep and suddenly from nowhere was attacked! He punched and kicked the servant girl. She punched and kicked him back. She was a plucky, feisty thing, it must be said. The muleteer came to save her once again. The innkeeper joined in.

All fought all, struggling, pounding in the dark: the innkeeper, the servant girl, the muleteer, and the squire. All fought all, not knowing even whom they fought. And then a voice that no one recognized came ringing through the dark.

"Stop in the name of the law. Shut the gates. See that no one leaves the inn. They have killed a man in here!"

Another lodger at the inn, a member of the countryside police, had heard the tempest raging up the stairs and, climbing them – unseen by all the others – had come upon the figure of Quixote bleeding and not moving on the bed. He'd caught Quixote by the beard to wake him. Quixote had not stirred.

The knight was dead.

Don Quixote Brews a Healing Balm;
A Blanketing

W as Don Quixote dead? You know that he was not. This is a book that bears his name and it is far from over.

Maritornes, the innkeeper, and the muleteer now fade into the borders of the tale. The countryside policemen retreated down the stairs to find a lamp.

Once again we find the knight and squire beaten into heaps of aching flesh, alone and in the dark. Awake this time and groping for each other with their voices.

From his shattered bed of pain – his broken bed – Don Quixote did his best to tell his squire how the fight had started. The princess: she had come to him to quench a lover's thirst. He'd had to turn the girl away. Their thwarted tryst was ended by a giant who hit him in the face. Perhaps the giant was enchanted by a Moor!

"A single Moor!" said Sancho. "I should have been so lucky! I have been beaten by four hundred Moors!"

Four hundred! That is so many! thought the knight. He turned this number over in his taxed and tired brain. "This castle," said the knight, "has been enchanted!"

They lay there, wondering at these events and not yet strong enough to move.

But rescue of a sort was on the way. The member of the countryside police returned carrying a lantern. He came to find the dead man and he was overjoyed to find the fallen figure come to life.

"You poor old thing!" he said, relieved and friendly, approaching with his lantern and a smile.

Was this stranger too familiar in his greeting? Did he fail to show the kind of quaking awe one might expect around a character as great as Don Quixote?

These, it seems, were Don Quixote's thoughts. From his bed, Quixote spat out insults for the man who'd taken such an interest in his fate.

"I would speak more politely if I were you," Quixote snapped. "Is this the way of locals to address knights-errant? You booby!"

The policeman raised his lamp and broke it over Don Quixote's head. He left the room.

All was dark and quiet once again.

"That was an enchanted Moor!" said Sancho.

Time passed. Dawn came. Finally, Quixote had a further thought. "Perhaps we need the legendary magic healing balm of Fierabras."

Of course!

From his place upon the bed, Quixote listed the ingredients that Sancho Panza must somehow find. Quixote knew exactly how the mixture should be brewed. This came from information in his books.

Sancho Panza, stalwart soul, rose and did as he was ordered. Enlisting help from other guests, he gathered all the elements of balm: the rosemary and salt, the oil and wine.

And then Quixote rose from bed as well. He poured and measured, cooked and mixed and brewed. He made perhaps two hundred prayers to bless the balm.

I think I will extend a warning to the squeamish. Perhaps you'd like to turn your eyes away. Perhaps you'll read this next part through your fingers.

Life is full of moments that fall well short of being pretty or polite. The next events will make this point quite nicely.

Quixote was the first to taste the balm. Drink it down he did in knightly gulps. Up it came in jets and gusts and spurts.

And then, his dinner spilled upon the floorboards, the knight fell into deep and restful sleep.

He slept three hours. He woke to feel refreshed. Success!

It was the squire's turn to try the cure.

Sancho Panza's stomach was not sensitive. The potion did not quickly reappear. Sancho drank the potion down, and down it stayed – or down it stayed at first. Down it stayed for long enough to make the squire well and truly poisoned.

Before the balm would make its way upstream, Sancho Panza wretched and gulped and struggled. The potion simply stubbornly refused to leave its lair within his poisoned gut.

Don Quixote watched the squire with growing interest – his patient who was wriggling and gasping on the floor. "Perhaps," he weighed this thought aloud, "this balm is only suitable to finer folk, like knights. Perhaps it will not work its magic on a humbler sort."

No sooner had he said these words when Sancho was volcanic at both ends. Volcanic he remained for two long hours. His suffering was very great. He suffered fore and aft. Need I give you details? The blankets and the mat on which he lay had later to be taken and destroyed.

There would be no healing sleep for Sancho, neither then nor through the night that came. The morning found the squire much the worse for all the wondrous healing he'd endured.

~∞~

On the other hand, daybreak found Don Quixote bustling with good health. A brand new day had dawned. The world was full of weak and full of needy, awaiting his stout heart and mighty sword.

Sancho Panza must get up and out of bed. And Sancho Panza did as he was told.

But before the knight and squire could leave the inn, another complication would arise.

Perhaps we should not put too fine a point on this, but there's a glaring instance now before us of how mean of spirit are the simple folk. How plodding and how piddling their concerns! The innkeeper had a matter to take up with Don Quixote. As the knight prepared to take his leave, the innkeeper inquired about his payment.

His payment? Don Quixote, naturally, was shocked. To begin with, as he patiently explained, he had understood this was a castle, not an inn.

"And furthermore," Quixote said, "even if this were an inn, knights like me are never asked to pay. We are sheltered free of charge, in thanks for all our service to the world. You are a stupid innkeeper," he said.

Don Quixote climbed upon his horse to leave the inn. He took with him a staff he found within the courtyard walls. It would do nicely as a lance. He rode out the gate on Rocinante.

Once again, his squire was not lucky. Poor Sancho Panza

was to pay a hefty price for Don Quixote's dignified escape. He paid with an indignity that all his days would be a bitter pill.

Having failed to get his payment from Quixote, the innkeeper applied to Sancho Panza for the sum. Like his master, Sancho Panza invoked the rules that governed knights and squires. If knights need never pay to spend the night, neither need their squires. And Sancho Panza would not be the one to change the rules.

Haughtily he climbed upon his ass. Haughtily he rode toward the gates on haughty mount. But fate would sweep his haughtiness aside. For there were other guests who sensed an opportunity for fun at his expense: four wool combers from Segovia, three needle makers from Cordoba, and two travelers from the markets in Seville. They pulled our squire from off his ass and hefted him above their heads, and threw him on a blanket in the yard. From the blanket they devised a trampoline.

Oh, poor beleaguered squire Sancho Panza. They threw the squire in the air, caught him in the blanket, tossed him up. It was a game that usually, and cruelly, was played with dogs on feast days. It therefore was no compliment to Sancho, and certainly no favor to his ravaged bowel.

How Sancho must have marveled, as he sailed into the sky, at the pass to which his new career had brought him.

How roundabout, this route to being king. As he flew he sent forth thoughts and prayers.

From atop his horse outside the walls, Don Quixote watched the squire rise and fall. He watched his servant come and go against the bright blue sky – sprawling like a starfish at one sighting, curled up like an infant at the next. Right side up, upside down, helpless and afflicted and unwell.

Don Quixote later told the squire he would have come to rescue him had Don Quixote not been himself enchanted. He didn't have the strength, he said, to scale the castle walls and save his squire.

Don Quixote Mistakes a Flock of Sheep for Armies; A Further Brush with Medicine

Hen they were on the road again, Sancho Panza had some matters to address about enchantment.

"I am persuaded," Sancho said, "that those who have amused themselves with me were not enchanted, but flesh and bone as we are. And you were not prevented from coming to my rescue by enchantment. And what I know from these events is that if we continue our adventures, soon we will not know our right feet from our left. The best and wisest thing would be to give up wandering from pillar to post, as the saying goes, and to go home. It's harvest time and there is work to do."

It turned out Don Quixote had also felt things could have gone much better. He was aware their enterprises had not all turned out as they might have hoped.

The good news was Quixote had an answer. He knew exactly what the trouble was. They only lacked a special kind of sword. It was a sword he'd read about – a weapon that had powers that enchanters would be helpless to confront.

Swords like this did certainly exist and here was proof: none other than Amadís had owned one. And he was the most famous knight of all! In fact, Knight of the Burning Sword was another of that great knight's knightly names. Now, would he have this title for no reason? Well, no.

Against this logic, Sancho Panza had no argument to make.

But talk of swords and blanketing and Amadís would have to wait. Up ahead, a cloud emerged – a roiling cloud of churning dust. Whoever stirred the dust could not be seen but Don Quixote knew full well what circumstances clouds of dust implied.

Up ahead, as plain as day to Don Quixote, there were two armies who were coming for each other head to head. As the cloud grew closer, he began to see the armies in detail – knights and giants, in the main, visible despite their being wholly hidden by the dust.

One warrior wore armor made of snakes and carried, for a shield, a sort of gate. Another rode a zebra and held a shield that bore an image of asparagus. He wore blue armor made of fur from squirrels.

Sancho Panza? He saw only dust.

Another knight bore a drawing of a cat upon his shield,

and just one word: Meow. It was a reference to his lady fair. And Don Quixote saw as well: a man dressed in a costume made of iron; others crowned with ears of corn; warriors with holes pierced through their lips.

Sancho Panza still saw only dust.

"There is no sign of anything you talk of," Sancho said. "No knight or giant. Maybe it is enchantment once again. Perhaps you see things that aren't really there."

"How can you say that?" asked the knight. "Do you not hear the neighing of the steeds? The braying of the horns? The roll of drums?"

Listen as he would, Sancho Panza heard none of this. He heard instead, the peaceful bleating of a flock of sheep.

It's difficult to know how Don Quixote imagined that what followed would give comfort to the needy.

He spurred on Rocinante, and leaving in his wake the shouted warnings of his squire, Quixote charged into the dusty flock, and speared his wooly foes to right and left.

And flock it was – a flock of sheep.

Of course their shepherds let out terrible shocked cries. What could they do to save their sheep from dying? They took up slingshots and sent the largest rocks that they could find, sailing through the air at Don Quixote.

There was a stone that met its mark, plunging into Don Quixote's chest. But Don Quixote, murderous and mad, was not deterred. He remembered that he had the magic potion – the balm he'd used with such success before. Somehow, in the tempest he'd created, he found a way to bring the bottle to his lips. He tipped it back, still stabbing all around him as he drank.

But as he drank, another stone flew up to find the hand that held the flask. It smashed the bottle and two fingers of his hand. It knocked out several of his teeth. He dropped from Rocinante to the ground. And so Quixote won the sort of victory that had become his trademark: he the victor on his back upon the ground.

The shepherds gathered up their dead and injured charges and set off in escape. Terrified, they thought the knight was dead.

Sancho bent down low to peer into his master's wounded face.

Perhaps you'd like to look away again? I'll warn you, what comes next is quite unpleasant.

His master, you'll recall, had only moments earlier drunk of the healing brew. It was just as the squire bent down that the magic potion made its upward journey out of Quixote's bleeding damaged maw.

We will not candy coat the truth. Quixote's dinner ended up in Sancho Panza's beard. Overcome, his stomach turned, Sancho Panza returned his master's volley. I'll try to put this gently. They each displayed their recent feasts upon the other's face.

Stinking and disgusted, the pair would need some nimble reasoning to think of this as any sort of triumph.

But Don Quixote, conqueror of sheep, would not be conquered by apparent facts.

"This has been a great and worthy battle, and with armies, not with sheep. Enchanters made the armies seem like sheep to try to rob me of my hard-earned triumph. But they have failed.

"These troubles that befall us," said Quixote, "are signs that better weather will come soon – that things will go well with us, for it is impossible for good or evil to last forever. Good fortune must be just around the corner.

"God, who gives us everything, will never fail us, for He does not fail the flies up in the air, the grubs who crawl within the earth, nor the tadpoles swimming in the water. The sun will rise on good as well as evil."

The Rescue of the Fallen Knight;
Don Quixote Gains His
Knightly Name

∽

Night came. The sky was dark and strewn with stars. Quixote and his squire made their way along the road, stars above and up ahead more stars – stars where there should not be stars. The stars grew larger.

Quixote and the squire stopped and peered into the twinkling dark. The stars that came toward them became torches. Holding them aloft were men in robes, and on their lips a low and mournful chant.

Closer. They came closer. A dark shape in their midst became a coffin. Sancho shook. Don Quixote's hair stood on its ends.

Were these strangers carrying a coffin? Or was their freight some sort of litter carrying a slain or wounded knight?

If the litter bore a knight in need, no weariness, no sickness, no injury, no coating of another man's old dinner would stop Don Quixote from offering his aid.

Don Quixote stood his ground. Sancho Panza's teeth began to clap. Don Quixote waited as the group approached.

"Where are you going on this road by dead of night?" he asked. "What do you carry? Why with torches? Why with chants and songs?"

One said, "We are in haste. We can not stop to give you the account that you demand." He spurred his mule.

In haste? What did they flee? And why refuse to answer simple questions?

"Halt and be more mannerly," said Don Quixote. "Otherwise you will taste of my wrath."

The men did not obey.

Once again, Quixote's knightly instincts lit a fire in his feeble frame. He raised his sword and flew into the twinkling, chanting group, nimble in his passion, a wasp, a scorpion, a spider stinging right and left, on them and among them all at once. And Rocinante, on this day, became the dancing steed that lived in books.

Surprise became Quixote's sharpest weapon. Caught off guard, his victims scattered with their torches to the hills. They scattered and they left behind their cargo, a coffin on the road.

They scattered all except for one who, pinned beneath his donkey, could not rise. He lay helpless on the ground. Quixote placed a knife point at his head and asked again,

"What is your business on the road?" The fallen man must answer to preserve his life.

He told the knight and squire he was a student and a man of God. The men Quixote had attacked were priests and mourners traveling from Baeza to Segovia to bury a man who'd died of fever on a journey. They were acting on the dead man's dying wish that he be laid to rest at home.

Was this a reason they should be attacked with swords?

In the dark, Don Quixote told the student that he was a knight. He had been meaning to right wrongs when he'd attacked.

"My leg is broken," said the student in response. "I am young, but I will never have its proper use again."

Quixote and his squire set the injured man upon his donkey and set him free to follow his companions.

Did sadness cross Quixote's battered features? Perhaps it did. He had meant well but he had done such harm.

Sancho Panza looked into his master's face and said, "You are the Knight of Mournful Countenance. This is how you seem tonight: your teeth knocked out, exhausted, underfed. I think your face the ugliest I've ever seen."

In truth, this wasn't meant to be an insult. Quixote did not take the least offense.

Said Don Quixote to the squire, "Many knights have special names like this. There is a knight who is He of the

Damsels. There is He of the Phoenix; He of the Burning Sword; Knight of the Griffin; The Knight of Death. I'll have a shield made up," he said. "I'll have it painted with the image you describe: a mournful countenance. And everyone will know my knightly name."

"You will not need it," said the squire. "They'll only need to see your face."

Then suddenly, the men were not alone. The injured student had returned. He'd not gone far. He'd only moved into the dark and now had something that he wished to say.

"You know," said he, addressing Don Quixote, "that you are excommunicated. You've put yourself outside the Christian Church. This is the punishment for attacking a priest."

This is the last we see of him – this student with the broken leg. He made his way into the hills, broken and brought low by Don Quixote's fevered and misguided act.

"And so," Quixote said, "now back to business. We shall look into the coffin at their cargo. Is there a full-fleshed corpse inside or only bones?"

Sancho did not wish to know and Don Quixote let the matter rest.

Instead, Don Quixote and his squire took what they could of all the food the priests had carried. And these were priests, their packs made plain, who took no vow of hunger.

The two set off. When they found a spot to rest, they ate four meals in one.

As they used to say: to the grave with the dead. To the living the loaf of bread.

TERROR IN THE MEADOW;
SANCHO PLAYS A TRICK AND TELLS A
TALE; A MYSTERY IS SOLVED

꒰ꔚꕤꕥ꒱

Their stomachs full of dinner, Don Quixote and his squire had to find a way to quench their thirst. They crossed a meadow lined with grass and reasoned that, with soft grass underfoot, there must be water feeding it close by.

The night was black. The stars had taken flight into the heavens. The meadow stretched ahead. Our heroes moved on slowly, blinded by the dark and apprehensive.

The wind picked up the way it does at night, hinting at the hidden places in the brush. It rushed toward them from the trees, plucked their clothes, ran through their hair, and whispered at the animals. It rustled and filled up our heroes' ears.

On they went. Pitch dark. And then, beyond the rushing leaves, roaring water, growing louder at each step so loud it was unnatural and strange.

Beyond the water, something more: a sound that made their chests contract with fear. A sound as dark as darkest dungeons, a sound like clanking chains, like pounding drums, a sound unceasing, rhythmic – like nothing Don Quixote and his squire had ever heard.

Don Quixote quickly sensed that there was danger to be met and overcome, and not far off. But even in the dark – without the benefit of looking into Sancho Panza's face – he knew the squire was far from in the mood for more adventure. And so Quixote settled on an answer.

"My heart bursts in my bosom through eagerness to go on this adventure," said the knight, "arduous as it promises to be. I will go ahead. Wait for me three days and nothing more. If in that time I don't return, you will go alone to El Toboso. Say to Dulcinea that her captive knight has died in attempting to be worthy of her love."

As plans go, this was sensible – exploiting all the knight's unflagging courage, allowing for the squire's flagging will. But Sancho Panza said it would not do.

It's possible Sancho Panza wanted to be included, just this once, among the knight's beloved weak and needy.

"I've given up my quiet, happy life," the squire said. "I've left behind the comforts of my home, my wife, and children. Do not desert me in this place so far from human reach.

Quixote would not listen. A knight can not indulge a squire's cowardice.

So Sancho Panza made a plan. Summoning each scrap of wit within his skull, he came up with a scheme to trick Quixote. He would not wait alone by dark of night. Secretly and deftly, Sancho took the bridle from his ass. Secretly and deftly, he tied Rocinante's two front legs together.

And so it was when Don Quixote bravely set his face toward the mysteries ahead, when Don Quixote finished his instructions and good-byes, when Don Quixote set his spurs to Rocinante to set off on what might well have been his final quest, the horse responded, not with a forward charge, but with a pointless bouncing up and down.

Don Quixote tried his spurs again. His armor clanked, the trappings flapped. The horse hopped up and down. Once more. No good at all.

The horse had been enchanted!

Thus did Sancho Panza have his way. Don Quixote had no choice. He'd wait. What could he do? Later he would try the horse again.

In the meantime, Don Quixote, vigilant, hearing every snapping twig and turning leaf, would stay up in his saddle. Knights do not need sleep. His horse's odd infirmity was no excuse. He'd sit there, upright, waiting for the moment when the spell would lift.

And Sancho? He wrapped both arms around Quixote's leg. To keep them both awake he told a tale, delivered into Don Quixote's thigh.

༄

There was a goatherd and he lived in Extremadura. His name was Lope Ruiz, and Lope Ruiz was in love. His loved one was the shepherdess Torralba. "She was," said Sancho Panza, "the daughter of a wealthy man."

But fortune had not smiled on her in all respects. She was unruly in her manner. She was plump. And she was somewhat masculine as well; she had upon her lip a little mustache.

Notwithstanding how eccentric were her assets, Lope loved Torralba. But she did not love him. Which is not to say she could not love. She could, and did, and often. But not this boy.

Mercifully for Lope, at last he ceased to love this girl. But Lope's love did not become indifference. As love so often will, it writhed and wrung within his heart. It wriggled inside out and turned to hate.

Before too long, he hated her ferociously. He hated her sufficiently to decide he would never lay his eyes on her again. He made a plan to leave, with all his goats, and flee to Portugal.

Meanwhile, in keeping with the physics of such things,

Torralba's suitor's new neglectfulness allowed her heart to thaw. She came to love the boy now that he did not love her.

In the perverse, unfailing logic of romance, the more the boy despised the girl, the more she loved. The more Torralba loved Lope, the keener was his longing to escape. She bored him with her weeping and her pleading.

And so, young Lope set about his trip. He crossed the plains of Extremadura. Three hundred goats were at his side.

But poor Torralba, she would not be shed. Taking her belongings – two saddlebags swinging from her neck, a mirror and a comb, and lotion for her face – she made off in pursuit.

He fled. She followed. On they went – he first, she trailing him through fields and brush and ditches.

And then he reached a river. How would he evade her now? How would he cross the river with his goats? How would he find a way to spare himself a lifetime of the girl's unwanted and mustachioed attentions?

And then, a ray of hope. At the riverside he came upon a fisherman who had a boat. The boat was big enough to take Lope Ruiz and just one goat.

He climbed into the boat. He took the goat across and came right back. Torralba had not come. And then he took another goat, and then another, and another. Such luck! No sign, still, of Torralba.

Now, at this moment of the story, Sancho Panza paused. In case he should lose count, he said, Don Quixote might be called upon to recall how many goats Lope had carried over to the other side. It was essential that the details be correct. If they lost track, he said, the story would be over.

And then the squire took up his tale again. The riverbank, he said, was wet and slippery. The landings on the other side were difficult. Back and forth the goatherd went. Once more. Once more. Once more. Once more. Once more. Once more. Torralba had not come, but surely it would not be long.

"And now," asked Sancho Panza, stopping to collect his thoughts, "remind me, Don Quixote. How many goats have crossed the river on the boat?"

The question seemed to come as a surprise. "How the devil do I know?" asked the knight above him in the saddle, annoyed to have the story interrupted. "Must you know how many goats have crossed?"

"Yes," said Sancho Panza, "and now that I find you've lost the count, the story has completely left my head."

"So then, the story's at an end?"

It was.

☙❧

We come now, on the journey through this book, to a detour – at least I will provide one. Straight ahead there is an anecdote with details some will find off-putting. There might be some who'd rather take a path around.

Readers who are squeamish or refined would be better off rejoining us in a page or so. The rest of us, of ruddy sensibilities, will plunge ahead.

Let me remind you. Before Quixote and his squire came upon the dreadful rhythmic pounding in the night – before there had emerged that dawning foretaste of this new and noisy danger – they had enjoyed, after fasting for some time, a feast. Four meals in one.

And we can take for granted that of this feast Sancho Panza would have had the lion's share.

So feast had followed famine, and in its wake Sancho Panza's bowels became as lively as the wind among the trees.

Sancho knew that he must do (and please forgive such bluntness) that thing that one can not do for another. And he knew he must do this right away. But how? He was too frightened to release his master's leg.

And so the squire was pressed into another secret act of sleight of hand. With every scrap of stealth that he could muster, in a feat of prestidigitation born of panic, silently and scarcely stirring, he untied the cords that held his pantaloons in place. He let them drop. He bent his legs. He stuck his great plump haunches out behind and undammed the mighty river of his guts.

It would be impossible to overstate the evils that this offered up to Don Quixote's nose.

"Sancho," said Quixote, "it strikes me that you are in terrible fear. You smell more strong than ever, and you do not smell of perfume." The knight raised up a trembling hand to stop his nose.

"I'll bet," said Sancho Panza, "that your worship thinks I have done something I ought not to have."

"We'll not discuss it further," said the knight. We will give Quixote credit for discretion. And we will leave the subject here as well.

⁂

The night wore on. The sun began to rise. Sancho Panza, quiet as a mouse, restored his breeches to their proper perch. Hurrying, for it would soon be light, he untied Rocinante's legs.

The darkness was dispelled but not the clanking and the rushing of the water up ahead. And not Quixote's willingness – no, eagerness – to meet whatever challenge it implied.

Quixote tried his horse. He found that Rocinante was now free to move.

So, onward! He would venture forth to face this task. Sancho Panza was to wait three days to be there if he should come back, and to take word to Dulcinea should he not. This was all the knight would ask of Sancho.

But Sancho Panza, now in tears, could not obey. He was afraid to stay alone, afraid to come along.

And so, as Don Quixote spurred his horse and made his way toward the dreadful sound, Sancho Panza crept along behind him, crouching down and peeking out through Rocinante's legs. Through the sturdy chestnut trees they went: ears straining and eyes bulging, hearts drumming and palms damp.

One mystery was quickly solved. They came upon a waterfall. This was the roaring water. But then, beyond the waterfall, and farther down the path, their frightened eyes fell upon a settlement of shacks; buildings more like ruins than like houses. From within these ruins came the clanging.

What living nightmares could these shacks contain? What creatures might await them, clanking chains? What could be taking place in there? Who doing what to whom?

They made their way downhill to the settlement, their hearts balled into fists.

Oh reader, do you expect to meet some mighty foe to justify the pluck it took to come this far?

Let me quickly put your fears to rest. The foe that knight and squire discovered in this lonesome spot was fulling mills, where wool from sheep was pounded day and night with heavy weights. The wool would soon be blankets and warm clothing. The pounding was a rhythmic clanging clamor. Unless you were afraid of wool, unless you were afraid of sheep or blankets, it was nothing to be frightened of. No giants were involved. No serpents. No unthinkable behavior was required. Nothing needed slaying in such a place by knights. No courage needed summoning to approach it.

Sancho Panza's joy was almost sumptuous. It's almost fair to say that he was giddy. Yes, Sancho Panza's mouth was full of laughter. But Sancho, although simple, was not stupid. He knew Quixote well enough to know he'd be chagrined by his mistake. And Sancho knew the laughter in his mouth had better stay there.

Sancho held his breath. He held his breath to keep from laughing. He puffed his cheeks. He did his best, but looked, for all the world, like he'd explode.

At the sight of Sancho's writhings, Quixote let a weak and rueful smile tilt his lips.

Sancho Panza could hold out no longer. He laughed. He laughed and laughed. He laughed until he cried. He laughed until he had to hold his sides to keep from bursting. He laughed although he knew that he should stop. He tried to stop. He stopped, then laughed again. Then stopped. And laughed.

Don Quixote lifted up his lance and brought it down on Sancho Panza's head.

The two moved on.

His merriment now much subdued, Sancho chose this time to ask what payment to expect for all his troubles. It's possible this easy-going fellow was annoyed. He'd heard, he said, of masters who apologize with gifts to servants they've mistreated. What might he anticipate for the clubbing he had just received? Perhaps they could discuss some sort of payment.

But Quixote had no patience for this peevishness. He told the squire that he would reap rewards that are described in books of chivalry. Had he not made this plain? Squires aren't paid wages week to week. Furthermore, Quixote said, he'd made some sort of mention of the squire in his will. Sheer generosity.

And one more thing, Quixote said, he'd thank his servant to keep his thoughts and questions to himself. Sancho must no longer chatter out his every passing thought. There was a squire in the books who – when he had good reason to address his knight – did so only with his cap in hand and eyes cast to the ground, bent forward, Don Quixote said, in Turkish style. This was a squire who showed his knight respect. Nowhere in the books were squires who prattled, barely pausing for a breath. "I blame myself," Quixote said, "for having let your insolence persist."

Sancho Panza, chastened, held his tongue.

THE HELMET OF MAMBRINO;
DON QUIXOTE TELLS HIS SQUIRE
OF THE LIKELY FATE OF KNIGHTS

Great adventures approach along the path of life if you have eyes to see them, as Quixote did.

On this day, there came another knight along the road and on his head there shone a golden treasure. Don Quixote knew it right away. It was the legendary golden helmet of Mambrino. And Don Quixote, in that moment, knew as well the treasure would be his.

Was fortune now about to go his way? Suddenly it seemed so. "Fortune might close one door," said the knight, "but not without its opening another."

The stranger came toward them. A knight upon a fine gray horse who wore atop his head a famous wonder: this is how things looked to Don Quixote.

To Sancho Panza, on the other hand, the figure up ahead was less imposing. Sancho saw a fellow on a mule, upon whose head there was an upturned bowl.

In fact – and now we'll set the record straight – the figure who approached was what was called a barber-surgeon. Such a man could give his customers a haircut and a shave, and then could cure their illnesses as well. He gave his patients cuts to let out blood.

In any case, it was a barber-surgeon who approached, wearing on his head a brand new basin to protect his hat from rain.

You'll guess by now, I think, what Don Quixote's strategy will be. He spurred on Rocinante. Mambrino's helmet blazed upon his adversary's head. Sancho Panza begged the knight to leave the man alone. Quixote did not listen. Quixote charged the stranger, aiming with his lance to run him through.

"Defend thyself, miserable being," called out the knight. "Or give to me what is my due!"

The barber-surgeon-stranger-knight – dumbfounded, unprepared, jumped down off his ass and ran away. The basin fell and clattered in the dust. Thus did Don Quixote win Mambrino's helmet.

But even Don Quixote conceded that as helmets go this one was really very like a basin. He tried it on. He turned it back and forth to make it fit. Clearly, this great treasure had been damaged. Clearly there were bits that had gone missing. Don Quixote would see it back in proper form. He would find a blacksmith in their travels. Until then it would balance on his head.

Sancho Panza took the packsaddle from off the barber-surgeon's mule. These were the spoils of the victory. Perhaps, asked Sancho Panza, he could take the beast as well.

He could not take the animal. According to a detail of the code, one can not take the animal unless the enemy falls from it in battle.

In any case, Don Quixote and the squire set off again. Rocinante chose the route.

Sancho's ass followed on behind the horse. A faithful friend, example to us all.

⟨⟨⟨⟩⟩⟩

And so the knight and squire won a victory. They traveled slowly, savoring the leisure they had earned. Is anything more satisfying than a job well done? Few things.

But Sancho Panza found a bone to pick. The worry that he raised was this: however great Don Quixote's victories might be, how could his master win the fame of knights in books? But for himself and Rocinante and the ass, there were no witnesses to Don Quixote's deeds. What good were splendid selfless feats when there was no one looking on and taking notes? And how – another practical concern – would Don Quixote's unseen feats advance his squire? How would Sancho Panza get his island?

But Don Quixote, patiently dispelling Sancho Panza's ignorance, found a way to put his squire's mind at ease.

They did not need their feats recorded day to day, he said. They need not place their faith in men who spend their hours licking nibs and scribbling with quills.

"The way a knight becomes well known," he said, "is this: He goes out in the world. He faces dangers and performs his conquests, he triumphs over evil, rights some wrongs, and then becomes renowned by word of mouth."

With Rocinante in the lead, setting the direction and the pace, the day provided Don Quixote ample time to go into a story of their future. He let the squire glimpse the sort of fame that knights like him would win.

"Let's say one day a knight comes to a castle," said Quixote. "Let's put this castle in some far-off place. Even if our knight had never seen this place before, he'd be no stranger to whomever made their home within its walls. They would have heard his name, attached by word of mouth, to many thrilling awe-provoking tales.

"Now, from afar they'd see him coming. Perhaps they'd see the helmet of Mambrino on his head." (We might as well admit this is Quixote.)

Who would come out to greet him? Probably the children would be first across the moat. Out they'd rush, chattering with joy, reaching up, perhaps, to touch the trappings of his horse, running back and forth between the knight and castle door, wishing both to greet the great Quixote, but also to be first to bring the news of his arrival to the king.

The king! He'd no doubt be the gladdest of them all. He'd have heard all the commotion from inside. Perhaps he'd been attracted to the window. And now he'd hurry forth, gleeful like the children. A king but no less an admirer of knights.

He'd kiss the hero on both cheeks, this happy king, and then invite him in. He must introduce the great knight to his queen at once! And of course introduce him to his daughter, the princess.

(For now, we'll put the matter of the lady fair aside. This is no time to catch our hem on details.)

The princess would be the fairest creature possible. At the moment of their meeting she would steal our hero's heart, and in that moment, lose her heart as well.

It might be on that very night that a great adventure would arise. Perhaps a hideous and tiny dwarf would come into the hall, followed by a lady and two giants. Perhaps this group would ask their guest to perform a task that seemed impossible, devised to be impossible to any but the very greatest knight.

But can you guess? Would he accomplish it? Of course.

The flames of love are fanned by victory. Romantic obstacles would rise up in the lovebirds' path, but hurdles would be overcome. Complications and predicaments would rise up and be conquered.

The knight would serve the king somehow in battle. He would return triumphant to the palace. The king would die. God rest his soul. The knight would then be king. His squire, finally rewarded as was promised, would find himself the husband of a servant girl, among the very fairest to draw breath. And he'd become a count.

(And Sancho's wife? What of her fate? Why, she would want her husband to be happy, would she not? And likely she'd feel out of place in castles.)

"All we must do," said Don Quixote, "is find a king who is at war, won't live too long, and has a lovely daughter."

"When I am count," said Sancho, "I will have a barber who will follow me from place to place, in case – just on a whim – I want to shave."

An Encounter with a Chain Gang

D on Quixote's next adventure started as he lifted up his eyes to see the road ahead.

Coming down the road there was a gang of twelve men tied neck to neck with chains. Two guards rode alongside and carried muskets. Behind them, two more guards accompanied on foot, carrying spears.

To Quixote, such enslavement meant injustice. He could not brook the sight of men in chains.

But Sancho Panza knew about the way that life is lived out in the world. He'd seen this sort of thing before and told his master that the men in chains were convicts, on their way to sea to serve their sentences rowing in the ships. These men were to be galley slaves, captives of the king – not victims of injustice, said Sancho, but criminals, paying for their crimes.

"Nonetheless," said Don Quixote, "we must know that all is as it should be." And so Quixote stopped the shackled men.

A guard confirmed what Sancho Panza'd said. These men had broken laws. But Don Quixote said he must know more. He asked to hear the stories from the prisoners.

And so the prisoners, stopped there in the road, gave answers – their answers more like riddles than like reasons for their punishments.

The first said he'd been put in chains because he was a lover. "A lover?" asked Quixote. And when did this become a crime? A lover! Perhaps Quixote should be put in chains himself.

"The love is not the sort of love you're thinking of," the man explained. "My love was for a washerwoman's basket of clean linens. I loved them well and carried them away. I've taken something else as well: one hundred lashes on my back and I will spend three years aboard the ships."

Don Quixote turned now to a second man in chains, who proved to be too downcast to give answers. The first prisoner spoke for him: "He goes to sea as a canary. He is a musician and a singer."

He was a singer? How did this break the law? "I have heard it said," said Don Quixote, "that singing heals the heart and dries the tears."

"Well, he was a singer of a sort," the first man said. He was a criminal who sang out under pressure from police. He confessed to his wrongdoings. He admitted he was a cattle thief. He was hated by the others for his weakness.

He'd had two hundred lashes with a whip, with six years in the galleys to be served. Hard time among his enemies on board.

A third explained he was in chains because he'd wanted for a small amount of money. He was in chains for poverty? Barbaric! "Yes," he said. "For poverty!" He could not pay for lawyers and for the bribes for judges. He could have bought his freedom if he'd somehow had the means to pay them off. He'd not be, as he told the knight, "chained up like a grayhound on the road."

The next in line – a fellow with a long white beard – was too distraught to speak, and another convict spoke on his behalf. He told Quixote that this man had been arrested as a matchmaker. He made his living pairing men and women. "Well," said Don Quixote, "you were arranging for the happiness of others! Surely this is not against the law!"

The truth is that the bearded man had not been pairing couples to be married, but for unions of a briefer and less binding kind. And furthermore, he had been dabbling in the arts of witchcraft.

The matchmaker wept bitter tears. He told Quixote he was now so old and having so much trouble with his urine that he did not expect to stay alive for long. Quixote gave the man a little money from his purse and moved along.

The next man, most unsavory, told of his misdeeds with his girl cousins and two other girls. He said that they had carried on their "joke too far." About his sense of humor and the details of this comedy we'll ask no more. We'll only say he'd twisted up the family tree. He would row for six years on the ships.

And finally, a criminal who claimed he was a student – a prisoner who stood out from the rest. He was well dressed not only as to clothing, but in extra chains as well. Another thing: his eyes turned in, regarding one another. This prisoner, so said the guard, was guilty of more crimes than all the rest together.

This cross-eyed prisoner did not describe his crimes but did reveal that while he'd been in prison in the past, he'd written down the story of his life. A writer. His plan was to continue this on board the ships. He'd been a galley slave before and did not fear his punishment at all. This prisoner was not afraid of galleys or of guards. And he was not afraid of Don Quixote. He demanded that Quixote move aside and let them pass.

And so the knight was faced with a decision. Did these men deserve their sorry fates? Don Quixote decided they did not. No. The knight would rain his mercy down upon them.

He asked the guards, would they be good enough to please release the captives? At first he asked as nicely as he could.

The guards of course, would not undo the chains.

Don Quixote's charge went off so suddenly that all the guards were caught, let's say, off guard.

But soon enough they found their feet and came at Don Quixote with their weapons. Indeed, they might have finished off the knight if, in the fight that followed, the prisoners had not escaped their chains.

The battle turned. The criminals were freed.

Don Quixote – liberator – bid the happy convicts gather round. He had a boon to ask – a way that these good men could show their thanks. He said that they should go to El Toboso. They were to pay a call to Dulcinea, to tell her that their freedom had been accomplished bravely in her name.

Whatever wisdom there might have been in sending twelve convicted criminals to pay a visit to his Dulcinea, he would not see it done. They would not risk their liberty, they told him. They'd scatter off to freedom in the hills.

"To ask this of us," said the cross-eyed student-convict, "you might as well ask pears to drop from elm trees."

Stupefied and furious, enraged at this ingratitude, Quixote hurled forth insults at the men. They answered him with stones.

Don Quixote and his squire, Rocinante and the ass were driven to their knees and to the ground. The criminals took Sancho Panza's clothes. They left him nearly naked in the dust.

The student-convict took Mambrino's helmet from Quixote and bounced it off his liberator's head. Rocinante lay beside his master. The donkey shook his ears in disbelief.

The criminals ran off into the distance.

ᴓᴍᴩ

Do you remember at the inn, the man who stopped the fight up in the hayloft – the member of the countryside police?

His group went by the name "The Holy Brotherhood." It was a fraternity that roamed the Spanish roads to uphold the law. Sancho Panza knew they would not smile on knights and squires who went about the roads unleashing criminals. Sancho Panza, as we've seen, was worldlier than his *hidalgo* master, and with The Holy Brotherhood in mind, he insisted that the two be up and on their way. No time to lie about in pain today.

And though Quixote would not flee from any fight or from The Holy Brotherhood, or anybody else, he did agree to mount his horse and did not quarrel with the destination Sancho had in mind: off the road, as deep as they could go into the hills.

To Sancho Panza he said this: "You are a coward by nature, but lest you call me obstinate, this once I'll do your bidding. We'll withdraw before the danger that you dread."

Don Quixote and His Squire Find a Suitcase; They Meet a Wild Stranger

⟨⟨⟨∽⟩⟩⟩

Their next adventure gets its start not with a brewing battle but with a clue.

Don Quixote and the squire were following a path into the mountains when they spotted something partly hidden in the scrub along the trail. Quixote stopped and poked it with his spear. He pried it loose.

A suitcase.

The suitcase, from the look of it, had been there for some time. Its sides were rotted by the sun and rain, so rotten that there was no need to open up the case to look inside.

Inside the case were four white shirts, some further bits of linen, a handkerchief that had been filled with coins, and finally, a book.

Sancho took the linens and the coins. At long last, here was payment for his trials. Don Quixote agreed that this was proper. What to some might seem like theft was within chivalric code.

Of interest to the knight, though, was the thing that could neither be spent nor worn. Don Quixote set about examining the book, which offered up, in scraps of notes and phrases, the traces of a badly broken heart. Its author was a disappointed lover. He'd left the larger world behind, taking only poems and his musings and the letters he had written his beloved.

How had his belongings wound up in the bushes by the trail? If he had been met by thieves they would certainly have made off with the coins, Sancho pointed out. Whenever did our squire become so clever?

Puzzled and, in Sancho's case, enriched, the knight and squire resumed their winding course.

But peace was not to be their new companion.

Suddenly, from out of who knows where, there leapt into their path a fearsome creature. Was it a man?

It was a man, but only just. He looked like he was scraps of skin and bone – half naked, with bits of clothing hanging here and there upon his blistered flesh. His hair was long and tangled. He wore a long and tangled filthy beard. He jumped from rock to rock, springing on his feet, as much at home on rough terrain as any goat. He jumped from rock to rock and then he vanished.

Don Quixote guessed this was the author of the letters. Here was weak and needy to be comforted. They must find this weak and needy man. Don Quixote's breast was all aflutter in anticipation of a proper quest.

On they went into the hills. And then, along the mountainside, deep in a ravine, they found a mule.

The mule, still decked out in its saddle, was long dead, and had been lunched upon by passing beasts. Wild dogs had taken much of what had been this creature's flesh. The birds skipped merrily upon him, even now. The insects helped themselves. In the wilderness a corpse is always cause for celebration.

Don Quixote and his squire stopped. They gazed upon the beast. What were their thoughts?

Perhaps the knight – considering this body that had now become a banquet – considered too the awesome mysteries of life and death a rotting ass calls up.

The squire? More likely he still dwelled upon the happy accident of pilfered shirts and coins. Perhaps the sight reminded him to reach into his pack to find a bite to eat. Sancho's thoughts always bent more toward his dinnertime than destiny.

Whatever were their musings, we leave them in the dust along the trail. For coming down the path there was a flock of goats and then a goatherd. Don Quixote called out to the stranger. Once greetings had been offered and received, the goatherd shed some light upon the matter of the fallen mule.

He told them of a young man who had come up to the mountains half a year ago. He was well dressed, well spoken, and well mannered at the time. He rode the mule and brought along a suitcase.

"We saw this case," said Sancho, "and of course we did not touch it."

"Nor did I," the goatherd said. "The Devil is too clever. Things rise up from underneath one's feet to make one trip and fall."

When next the man was spotted in the mountains, said the goatherd, his appearance and demeanor were much changed. The fellow'd left behind his mule and suitcase and any traces of the gentleman he'd been. He was deranged and gibbering, and he'd rushed out at a fellow goatherd from behind some rocks. He beat the man and kicked him. He stole his bread and cheese and rushed away.

Misdeeds like this cannot be overlooked. The goatherds could not leave him running loose, making victims of their brethren in the hills. A band of goatherds searched for him. They found him huddled in a hollow tree.

The madman's face, by now, was tanned and torn by sun. He showed the strain of suffering and living unprotected in the hills.

But for all his wear and tear, he had become a tamer self again. He was sorry he had done the goatherd harm and vowed that when he needed food, he'd simply ask.

The wild man, the goatherd said, told the goatherd posse he would change his ways and, having made this vow, began to weep. He broke down in big, salty tears. He wept a broken-hearted flood.

The goatherds could do nothing but join in. One and all, they wept among the rocks, most of them not knowing why.

But soon enough their tears would stop and dry.

The madman ceased his sobbing. A new expression crossed the creature's face. He blinked his eyes and arched his brows and pressed his hard and sunburned lips together. The goatherds stopped and watched and held their breath.

And then the madman said these word: "Fernando. Now you'll pay the price for all you've done. These hands will tear your heart from in your chest!"

The madman leapt up to his feet and found the nearest goatherd and wound his fingers round the fellow's neck. No more the tender weeping version of himself, the madman would have wrung the life from his poor victim – would have bitten him and beaten him to death – had not the other goatherds held him back.

Swept back into lunacy and then into the trees, the madman danced off down the trail, near naked, spewing threats and curses, and was gone.

And so it had been ever since: violent at one encounter, gentleman the next. He'd lived there in the mountains these six months: appearing, disappearing, more ragged, unpredictable, and roasted by the sun at every turn.

Now, as our characters considered these events, as Don Quixote's wish to offer what he could to this unhappy soul became more firm, from out behind the rocks, the very subject of their talk appeared.

He mumbled words. His eyes rolled here and there. But he was calm and cordial and civilized and even warm. Given this, and given his most obviously wretched state, the meeting of the men was most affectionate.

Don Quixote made the introductions. He was a knight – noble, brave, extraordinary, all those things. He explained it was his mission to bring comfort to the suffering. Whatever he could do to be of help he would. But what had brought this fellow to such straights? He clutched the poor young man in an embrace.

The youth agreed to tell the group his tale. He would tell it, but under one condition. The listeners must never interrupt.

THE WILD STRANGER'S TALE BEGINS

The youth was named Cardenio and as we might have guessed from the fancy sorts of things that he'd discarded, he was the son of wealthy parents – a boy who'd had good fortune on his side.

He was, as we have also guessed, in love. Can this be called good fortune? We shall see.

The object of his love was named Luscinda. She was the child of wealthy parents too, and beautiful and good. And she had loved Cardenio as well.

In fact the two had been in love since childhood. They'd grown up with no question as to what their fates would be. Both of them assumed they would be married and one day they decided it was time.

Both families had always looked most kindly on the match. It seemed there was to be a happy ending.

But life is not so simple; nor are stories. (Otherwise they'd all be much too short.) And so, to get the wedding underway!

According to the custom of the time, Cardenio would speak of his intentions to his father. It was the father's task, if he approved, to seek agreement from the father of the bride. What could go wrong?

Cardenio paid a visit to his father and, on the day he chose, found him in the sunniest of moods. But before the would-be groom could raise the subject of his hopes, his father had some news to share.

That very day he had received a letter from a nearby Duke. It was good news for Cardenio, or so it seemed. Good news, in fact, for all.

The Duke was called Ricardo. He was a most important man and he had written with an offer for Cardenio. He offered him employment as companion to his son. The offer was an honor and a compliment and an invitation to the sort of life that promised any number of advantages. If all went well, the letter said, the Duke would give Cardenio some fitting rank.

Cardenio, no fool, quickly saw that he and his Luscinda, would both reap the rewards of this position. Their marriage would take place in time, of course. They only needed to postpone it for a while.

And so Cardenio left home and took up life within the household of the Duke. As the Duke had guessed, Cardenio was nothing but a pleasure to them all.

What the Duke did not foresee was that it would be his second son and not his first who formed the closest ties with this young man. But this was of no consequence. Fernando, the second son, and Cardenio became the best of friends.

Don Fernando seemed to be exactly what a fine young man should be. He was noble. He was generous. He was gallant and affectionate and handsome. He was confiding too, and this is an endearing trait.

But among the confidences Fernando shared with his new friend were secret thoughts that called some of his virtues into question.

Don Fernando was in love as well. His beloved was the daughter of a farmer. The girl was not as highborn as was he – not a girl whom he'd expect to marry, but she was wealthy in the many things that nature can bestow. She was beautiful, industrious, and chaste.

It was this latter attribute – her chastity – that Fernando was anxious and determined to besmirch.

His plan was this: he'd promise he would marry her. So virtuous she was, said he, there was no other means to have his way. This was the secret he confided to Cardenio. Don Fernando knew that his intentions as regarded this young girl were wrong. And Cardenio, quite properly, agreed.

The two young men decided that Fernando must be taken from temptation. They would remove themselves to Cardenio's home town. They'd tell the Duke that they must go there to purchase horses. The horses in those parts were very famous.

And this they did.

But, as confiding as Don Fernando seemed, there was a secret he had not revealed. What Don Fernando did not confess was that his mission to besmirch this girl was one that he had already accomplished.

There had been an evening when his aims were met but since that night, his longing for the girl (as happens very often, please be warned) had turned into a longing to escape. While Cardenio had thought their trip was Don Fernando's fleeing from temptation, Don Fernando, secretly, was fleeing from his victim and his crime.

And so, the two great friends, one misleading, one misled, arrived in Cardenio's home town.

Cardenio did everything to show his friend the sort of hospitality that he'd enjoyed. He welcomed him into his home and told Fernando all about Luscinda and of their lifelong love and plan to marry.

He took his friend to stand beneath her window to behold her. He talked of her intelligence and wit. So proud was he, he showed his friend her letters. In fact there was one letter, in which she'd asked Cardenio to find for her a book she much admired. The book was *Amadís de Gaula*, and the reason she especially wished to read this book again . . .

Amadís de Gaula! Don Quixote, who had been silent all this time and listening, was ignited with delight to hear the name. Amadís de Gaula! None other than the greatest knight of chivalry. None other than the greatest knight of all.

"If you had told me that the lady had a taste for works of chivalry I would have needed no more proof that Luscinda is the flower you describe! And I can recommend to her all sorts of works she might enjoy! There are many books that I can give you. Mind you, an enchanter has made something of a dent in my supply. . . ."

Whatever Quixote found to say next about his favorite subject in the world is beside the point. The point is this: Quixote had done the very thing Cardenio had made him promise he would not do. He'd spoken in the middle of the story.

Cardenio let his chin drop to his chest. He looked as though he were absorbed in thought. And then it was his turn to interrupt. He raised his voice and halted Don Quixote in his tracks with a statement that was perfectly composed to start a fight – a vulgar slur against one of the fairest queens described in all of chivalry.

This queen, he said, had been the willing mistress of a

ne'er-do-well. The happy baggage of a low-born knave. He made this charge and he would not back down.

Well, Quixote could not ignore the insult! Cardenio dared tell a lie like this? He dared impugn the honor of a queen? Quixote would not have it. He would not!

As Don Quixote sputtered protestations, Cardenio raised a rock and hit him in the chest. The fight was on.

Sancho Panza came to Don Quixote's rescue. Cardenio threw Sancho to the ground. He jumped upon the squire's chest and leaped about on Sancho Panza's ribs.

Cardenio, fully now his other fearsome self – the self of blinking eyes and warring fists – danced a little punishment upon the fallen squire, then scuttled off and vanished in the trees.

"We must follow!" Don Quixote said. "We must find him. I wish to hear the ending of the tale!"

The goatherd – who can blame him? – took his leave.

DON QUIXOTE DECIDES
HE WILL GO MAD

⌘

The knight and squire did not go forth to find the madman right away. Knights have many duties. Another would take precedence this day. Don Quixote would go mad for love. It was a time-worn pastime of knights-errant.

Quixote explained to Sancho Panza that knights in books are very prone to lunacy, brought on by the agonies of love. Driven from their senses by their anguish, responding to an unrequited love or jealousy or feelings of betrayal or the like, they take themselves away to far off places. There they throw away their clothes and rampage in a frenzy of despair. They pull up trees. They murder goatherds and cut down their flocks. They burn down huts and prance about as though they are possessed by evil demons.

"And let us admit it," said the knight, "this is a simpler

way to imitate great knights than slicing giants into bits, killing dragons, sinking fleets of ships, and crushing armies."

"It seems to me," said Sancho, "that these knights you speak of are driven to madness by misfortune. What cause have you for madness? What lady has rejected you? What proof is there that the Lady Dulcinea has trifled with some rival? None at all."

But ingenious Quixote had an answer. "If madness for good reason shows the greatness of a knight's romantic love, how greater is his passion if he goes mad when he is unprovoked?"

There was a part to play for Sancho in this drama. His role would be messenger. Sancho was to go to El Toboso to find the Lady Dulcinea and tell her of Quixote's sorry state. He was to take a letter to the lady and bring an answer back to give the knight.

As to the letter he would send, Quixote said, they really needn't worry what it said. As far as he remembered, his lady fair could neither read nor write.

"She is a sheltered little flower," said Don Quixote. "There are so many things she's never seen or done, protected by the parents who so love her – her father, Lorenzo Corchuelo, and her mother, the good Aldonza Nogales."

Did Quixote say her father was Lorenzo? Her mother was Aldonza? Could it be? Sancho Panza recognized the names. They were the parents of the peasant girl, Aldonza. Aldonza Lorenzo – this was she, the girl who was the lady of his master's thoughts? Aldonza Lorenzo! Why, Sancho Panza knew the girl quite well! Everybody knew this girl, Aldonza.

"Why, she's a wonder," said the squire. "A great big strapping girl! She could pull a knight out of a mud hole. As brawny as a horse. And lungs! Her voice is like the bellow of a cow! I've seen her call in hired hands from miles away. She flings a crowbar like the strongest boy.

"And not at all the type to put on airs. Always one to slap her knee and laugh. And very friendly with the boys! Not prudish, that is for sure!

"And, by the way, she has no match for field work," he went on. "There's a lot of hair on that girl's chest. Not too bad at all.

"By now," he said, "I shall bet her face has seen much better days. All that work outside, it takes a toll. But still . . ."

Sancho fell silent. Misgiving creased his brow. "Is she the sort of lady fair one finds in books?" he asked the knight.

This lusty laughing lass? This brawny, brawling game, and goodtime girl? Was she the sort who would best suit the delicate attentions of a knight?

"Be quiet," said Quixote. "Do you think that all the ladies fair in books were as they were described? Do you believe that each and every one really existed? How typical of you, Sancho Panza, to miss the point completely! The lady fair is what the knight requires her to be."

Ingenious.

Before the squire was to leave, Quixote planned three days of madness. This would give his messenger a tale to tell to lovely Dulcinea. He would tear off all his clothes before the squire, scatter all his armor on the ground, knock his head against the rocks – this sort of thing. In short, he'd be unhinged by tragic love.

As to the letter for his lady fair, that strapping lass with wind worn face and loud and laughing lungs, Don Quixote wrote this note:

> Sovereign and exalted Lady,
> He who is pierced by the sword of absence, he who is wounded to the heart's core sends you, Dulcinea, the health that he does not enjoy. My good squire, Sancho, will relate to you in full, beautiful, cruel one, dear enemy, the condition to which I am reduced by my love for you. If it be your wish to give me relief, I am yours. If not, by ending my life I shall satisfy your cruelty and my desire.
> Yours 'til death,
> The Knight of Mournful Countenance.

"I'll get an answer out of her," said Sancho, "even if I must give the girl a hearty kick."

Having finished off his paperwork, Don Quixote stepped out of his breeches and his shirt. Naked as a newborn babe, he jumped into the air. He made cartwheels to show the sort of madness the squire should describe to Dulcinea.

Sancho Panza, horror-struck by these unwelcome views of Don Quixote, mounted Rocinante and rode off down the trail.

Alone at last, Don Quixote left off capering. He retreated up the rocks. How to begin? Should he begin by weeping? Maybe he would take up weeping later. Would it really be of use to pull up trees? Perhaps. But now? He'd lots of time to weep and pull up trees.

He finally decided he would pray. He'd pray fervently, and many prayers. He gathered up his shirttail and tied it in eleven knots to count his prayers.

But just a moment! There was something missing.

In a perfect world there would be a hermit standing by to serve as witness. Hermits in the books made note of sufferings and listened to confessions. There were no such secretaries here. He would have to suffer unregarded. This was not, and never is, ideal.

He settled down to dream up anguished poems. These poems he would carve into the trees.

Of the verses he composed thus in his madness, very few examples still remain. They are poems of such quality that scholars have not wrung their hands that most of them are lost to moss and time.

Sancho Panza Meets Some Old Friends; A Plan to Save Quixote; The Wild Stranger Finishes His Tale

⊙⫘⫘⊙

ancho Panza set out to deliver Don Quixote's letter to his lady fair.

But Sancho would not find his way to El Toboso. Instead, he found himself, within a day, in a place he'd visited quite recently, the inn that had been the site of his illness, the place where he'd been tossed up in the blanket. Once he recognized the inn he stopped the horse. The sky above grew dark.

Sancho was torn between two choices. If he were to go inside he would find dinner and a place to spend the night. If he were to stay outside the inn, he would be spared the company of people who had seen his great indignity.

Sancho did not know what course to take. He waited there outside the inn as night approached. And then, to his astonishment, two familiar figures came out of its doors.

It was the priest and barber, Don Quixote's friends from home, the men who'd brought down verdicts on his books. This was a happy, happy chance, to run into each other far from home.

But it was not entirely coincidence. In the hearty greetings that followed, came news the barber and the priest had come in search of their befuddled friend, Quixote. Everyone was worried sick at home.

And so the priest and barber's befuddled friend's befuddled squire brought the priest and barber up to date on their adventures, and on the many things the future held. He told them that Quixote would most likely be an emperor or king, that he would gain some rank himself, and maybe a new wife! His own – God rest her soul – might easily by that time have passed on. It's sad but true that no one lives forever.

He told them of the meeting with Cardenio and of Quixote's current love-struck state. He told them of his mission to the lady fair and of the letter that – he realized it now – he'd left behind. Sancho had committed it to memory.

"'Exalted and scrubbing lady, the wounded and wanting of sleep and the pierced kisses your worship's hands, ungrateful and very unrecognized fair one,'" he recited. "And it said something," Sancho said, "about health and sickness and it tailed off from there."

When his account of these adventures was complete, Sancho had a favor he would ask. Would the priest and barber bring him dinner from the inn? He couldn't do this for himself, for reasons he'd explain some other time.

They did, and Sancho Panza dined beneath the stars.

By morning, the priest and barber had devised a plan to lure Quixote home. The two described their scheme to Sancho Panza. The barber would dress up as a damsel. He would be a damsel in distress. They'd think of something that the lovely barber-damsel in distress would ask the knight to do. A favor of some kind. They knew the knight would not refuse a lady. The priest would act the part of damsel's squire. They would lure Quixote back toward La Mancha. Once there, they'd find a way to cure his madness.

When the three departed from the inn, they had costumes they would put on when the time was right. The priest, dressed as a squire, would wear a beard of oxtail – a clay red beard down to his waist. This oxtail was donated by the innkeeper. He used the oxtail, in the custom of the day, to store his combs.

The landlord's wife – generous in spirit and in size – had a frock that neatly fit the barber. He'd wear her woolen skirt, a white and green bodice, a bonnet, and a wide-brimmed hat, every bit as wide as an umbrella, and silk to drape about his forehead and his face.

With Sancho Panza in the lead, Quixote's friends retraced the squire's path, eventually arriving at a clearing by a riverbank, not far from where the squire had left the knight. The priest and barber put on their disguises: huge damsel, oxtail-bearded squire.

Sancho Panza left them there to rest and went ahead to find Quixote.

⌒⋙⋘⌒

The priest and barber didn't have to wait for long for fate to come and offer up diversions.

They heard a voice, cultured and refined – not the sort one might expect from goatherds – a voice that didn't match the rustic scene. The lovely voice was raised up in song.

The song was sad, and at its end there followed another. This was a tale of friendship lost, of promises abandoned, love betrayed. And then the voice left off its song, collapsing into jagged sobs and moaning.

Naturally, our characters were not content to wonder at the source of all this grief. They made their way downstream toward the wailing and, rounding a great rock in the ravine, they saw ahead a small and sunburned figure. They knew it was the man whom Sancho had described to them the night before. Ragged, thin, and wild he was. Cardenio.

They came out from behind the rock to greet him.

The priest and barber told the youth they knew of him. How could they be of help? What could they do?

Of course, you know that nothing will undo the past. Cardenio affirmed this; there was no point in offering their help. His darling childhood lover had been stolen. There was no happiness ahead for him. Not in this world. Not in the next. All ahead was blackness and despair.

Beside the stream, Cardenio retold his tale.

We'll join in at the place he stopped before.

⁂

You'll remember that Cardenio and Don Fernando had been great friends. That Don Fernando had confided all his longings for a virtuous and lovely local girl. He told his friend about his wayward appetites, but he did not confide that they'd been fed.

The two young men had left the household of the Duke to visit Cardenio's home. They would buy horses, so the story went. Once at home, Cardenio had made a trusting gesture and told Fernando about his love, Luscinda.

If only we could step into the book and tell the characters a thing or two we'd have them know. Don Fernando, as we've seen, could not be trusted. We know this, but

Cardenio did not. And so we will look on and wring our hands as Cardenio sets about his own undoing.

Smitten to the core and too confiding, he told Fernando of Luscinda's charms. He spoke of her intelligence and beauty. He brought his friend to see her at her window and let him read the letters she had sent.

There are few greater pleasures than to speak of a beloved. When one's in love the lover's name appears in every sentence as a rule. It's a pleasure that we'll wish Cardenio had resisted. He made his case too expertly, and soon Fernando loved the girl as well. He started plotting for her hand.

Fernando needed money to buy horses, so he said. Would Cardenio be good enough to go back to the household of the Duke and fetch the money he would need? Cardenio, of course, was most obliging. He left his home to undertake this business, and Don Fernando undertook the underhanded business of his own.

Cardenio had been in the Duke's household just four days when a stranger knocked upon the door. The stranger bore a letter for Cardenio.

The note was from Luscinda. Don Fernando had asked her father for her hand. Her father had agreed. His daughter would be married to the son of a great duke. What father would not wish this? The wedding was to take place right away.

Cardenio – imagine all his torment – made off at once for home.

Too late. It was too late for anything but one last meeting with his lover at her window. One last time he found her where they'd met so many times. She wore her wedding gown, for this was the very hour she would marry. She had but time to tell him she still loved him. She had a dagger hidden in her dress. She would take her life before she'd ever take Fernando as a husband.

Cardenio, of course, was somehow comforted. Better that she die than that his darling girl be stolen from his arms.

But for now, music and the makings of a feast. There was to be a wedding! She must go. He would follow her and hide himself and watch.

In the wedding hall, the ceremony underway, he hid behind some hanging tapestries.

There he stood, Cardenio, straining eye and ear, witness as his world came to an end. "The night of my unhappiness set in," he said. "The sun of all my happiness went down." He looked on as Luscinda agreed to be the wife of Don Fernando.

"I do." She said.

I do?

How Luscinda brought herself to say these words we'll never know. We know, though, having said them, she swooned and fainted in her mother's arms.

The hall became confusion and commotion. Don Fernando rushed to tend his bride. But as Fernando took her in his arms, he found a note she'd hidden in her neckline. We'll not learn until later what it said.

And so Cardenio, his Luscinda now married to Fernando, fled the hall and fled the town and set off to the mountains on a mule.

When the mule dropped dead from exhaustion, our sorry lover traveled on by foot. He walked for days – climbing, senseless, hungry, leaving in his wake hopes and possessions.

On the day he was discovered by the goatherds, he'd been lying raving on the ground for days.

This is the story that he told the priest and barber, the gigantic damsel and her bearded squire. But listen! Another voice came drifting through the trees. Another voice that promised yet another tale.

THE FOURTH PART

The Stranger at the Brook

⟨ﬁﬁ⟩

Where were we? In the mountains, with the priest and barber all dressed up. And with Cardenio. Cardenio had been telling the story of the loss of his Luscinda. Once again his tale was interrupted, this time by a broken voice from somewhere close.

"Oh God," it said. "I have found a place that may serve as my grave. Woe is me! There is none upon this earth to give me counsel, comfort in my sorrow, or relief in my distress."

Hearing this, our characters approached the grieving voice. They found a peasant boy, slender, pale, and pretty.

Was it a boy, so pale and pretty, his feet like shining crystal in the stones? No. It only seemed to be a boy at first. He seemed to be until he raised his hands up to his cap and took it off.

Storybooks make much of hair: long tresses, shining gold, throwing all about them rays of sun, dark locks of depth and length and color to make the nighttime sky lack luster. The long hair that this youth let down was of the sort immortalized in stories, so lovely – glowing auburn – there aren't sufficient beauties to compare it to. Like harvest time? Like dancing, glancing flame? A flowing, glowing river to the rocky ground? It was, to reach the point at last, hair that made all too plain that its owner was indeed a girl who cooled her alabaster feet. It was a girl whose loveliness can hardly be described.

The priest, the barber, and Cardenio stepped out from the brush. They wished to help.

Imagine her surprise – this creature who had thought she was alone, singing of her sorrows in the mountains. Naturally, her impulse was to run away. She quickly gathered up her few belongings. But her feet were much too soft to run across the rocky ground. She had no choice. She would await her fate.

But she would learn these strangers were no danger, if maybe quite eccentric in their dress. She would learn they only wished to help her. They'd heard her song, of course. What could they do?

There was nothing anyone could do, she said. But she would tell her story. The damsel knew she must explain her circumstances, lest her presence here might seem improper.

The four sat down beside the bubbling stream.

DOROTEA'S STORY

◯

O nce she'd been the happiest of children. She was an only daughter, beloved by her parents, sheltered by devotion and attention.

In due time she was mistress of the household. She spent her days in industry, tending to the duties of the farm. Over time, she'd made her parents prosperous and proud. She'd taken on the hiring and the firing of servants, had overseen the pressing of the olives, the winery, the herds and flocks and hives. She was industrious and capable and modest. A credit to her parents who were tenants of a local duke.

She was, as well, quite beautiful. Though her parents did their best to keep her from the world's rapacious gaze, she became well known for this above all else.

She caught many an eye, this lovely girl, among them those set in the handsome head of the Duke's own second son, Don Fernando.

Does this name ring a bell? It did for our Cardenio. His blood began to burn within his veins. His brow began to glisten when he heard it. His face turned pale. Could this be the Fernando who'd betrayed him and stolen his Luscinda?

Cardenio found a way to hold his tongue and let the girl go on.

Fernando, so the girl explained, had mounted a campaign to win her favors. Each day was like a carnival outside her door, for all the entertainments that he sent. At night no one could rest. Beneath her window ceaseless serenades were sung. Gifts and money flowed into her household – for the girl, her parents and the servants.

He bribed her maid to bring his letters to the girl. The letters made her every sort of promise, paid her every sort of compliment, and spelled out every sort of torture that the lovesick author suffered at her hands.

But for the many pains of Don Fernando, our storyteller did not lose her heart.

Nor could he make headway with her parents. They were the sort who truly loved their daughter – by which I mean who put her interests first. They had no wish to persuade her of the match, however much advantage they might reap. She should marry whom she wished and loved, they said. Finally, a rumor swept the town. These parents sought another husband for their child. They wished to put an end to all this courtship.

And so it was that Don Fernando opted for a final drastic ploy. One night, he found a way into her chambers.

For Don Fernando to do this was impossible. It could not be. But there he was. Had he, perhaps, paid money to her maid to leave the doors unlocked?

He took our storyteller in his arms. She was too startled to resist his grasp. Holding her against him, Fernando repeated all the contents of his letters. He told her of her beauty and of his despair, and he made promises.

He'd marry her, he said. But she must end his agony of love that night. She must gratify a bridegroom's wish.

On and on he rambled, wept, and begged. Our storyteller's mind began to reel. She knew that she could not escape his grasp.

And there was something else she knew as well. There was a chance they might be discovered. How would she explain? And what if he should force himself upon her? Who would believe her story when she told it? He was the Duke's own son, and she a peasant. In the eyes of all the world she would be ruined. Any girl would know this all too well.

And then a terrible disaster! His arguments began to hit their mark. Our storyteller's heart began to soften. Finally and fatally, her tender soul ceased to resist his pleading. She felt pity, and then felt something else: the rustling of a gathering emotion, the stirrings of what blossomed into love.

And so the girl agreed to an arrangement: if in the presence of her maid he would agree to marry – such promises were binding in those days – then he would have the privilege of a bridegroom. He would have the favors that he sought.

She called her maid. Don Fernando made his vows, the three watched over by a relic of the Virgin. Oh Virgin! Could you not step in to save her?

On that night Dorotea, without a marriage or a ring or vows, became a bride. A bride of sorts. At least in one respect.

Dorotea? Is this what she had called herself? Cardenio knew this name as well, of course. This was the local peasant girl Fernando had once told him of.

The storyteller went on with her tale. When morning came, it seems that Don Fernando's love had cooled. His longing for the peasant girl, once sated, had quickly died. He left his demi-bride a ring but took his cold heart with him.

He left the bridal chamber before sunrise.

The next night he returned. But not the next. Time passed. And then one day fair Dorotea learned that Don Fernando had been married. He'd been married to a woman in another town. Luscinda.

Dorotea didn't notice that Cardenio's eyes were wet with tears. The storyteller went on with her tale.

When Dorotea heard the news of Don Fernando's wedding, she found her breast was filled with more than sorrow.

She was, she now discovered, full of rage. She would hold her cheating bridegroom to his promises. She would find him and would call him to account. He would admit his villainy at least.

Dorotea sought help from a shepherd boy, who gave her a disguise. She dressed up as a shepherd. Together they left home to find Fernando.

Arriving in Luscinda's town, Dorotea heard the details of the wedding. The town was in an uproar. The story was on every pair of lips.

Do you recall the wedding of Luscinda and Fernando? It ended with Luscinda fainting in her mother's arms. Do you recall a note tucked in her neckline? Now we learn the contents of the note.

Written in Luscinda's hand, the note explained she could never be Fernando's wife. She was promised to Cardenio. Only he could really be her husband. Cardenio. He was her true and only love. He'd been so all her life and so remained.

Luscinda's groom, to say the least, did not accept the note with any grace. He found the dagger hidden in her clothing and he raised it up. If she would not be his, he'd take her life.

Luscinda's parents stopped his hand. Fernando fled the wedding hall and then the town. And then Luscinda disappeared as well.

But, back to Dorotea. Her parents had sent messengers to find her. All through the town there rang a public proclamation describing Dorotea head to toe, recounting that she'd run off with a shepherd.

Had anybody seen her, this girl whom they forgave and loved so dearly? She must be found and brought home.

But Dorotea could not go home. Her disappearance with the shepherd boy had been misunderstood. She was disgraced. She and the shepherd made their way into the mountains to seek the solitary life.

Secluded with the shepherd, she found she had to fend off his advances. One evil, as the saying goes, calls up another. Dorotea pushed him off a cliff.

Still in disguise, Dorotea found employment in the service of a herdsman. But soon he discovered she was not a boy and so she needed refuge from this man as well.

With no steep cliff to save her, she ran away and hid, at last, alone.

Oh, how we mourn the golden age – as Don Quixote had described it to the goatherds on that happy night beside their little fire: the golden age when women wandered free and, dressed in only leaves, were unmolested.

⊙〜〜〜〜〜〜〇

Thus did Dorotea's story end. Cardenio gathered up his ravaged thoughts and finally he found the words to speak.

He told the girl her life had more surprises still in store. He told her he, Cardenio, was Luscinda's true love. He made a pledge before her not to rest until their troubles were set straight. Cardenio would somehow find an answer.

Cardenio and Dorotea, the priest and barber marveled at these things beside the brook.

And then, a voice rang out from down the trail. It was Sancho Panza. The squire had returned.

Bad news.

The Plan to Save Quixote Is Advanced; A Scuffle over Dulcinea; The Beaten Boy

⚜

Poor dear Don Quixote. Sancho Panza'd found him in the lowest spirits possible. Quixote lay alone among the rocks – naked, yellow, skin and bones, weak from hunger, sighing for his Lady Dulcinea.

Sancho'd tried to rouse the knight by telling him his lady fair awaited him. He told him that he'd seen fair Dulcinea and that she dearly wished to see him.

But Don Quixote refused to stir. He would not accept her invitation. He had not yet achieved the sorts of victories required to make him worthy. He would not come. Not yet.

This was the news that Sancho brought the priest and barber, and now Cardenio and Dorotea too. There would be no simple way to bring Quixote home. The priest took Dorotea and Cardenio aside and told them of the plan they had come up with to take Quixote to La Mancha.

Dorotea listened and had an inspiration of her own. She, and not the barber, should play the damsel in distress, she said. She might be more convincing than the barber. What's more, she had the perfect costume with her – the finery she'd brought along from home. The barber would impersonate the lady's squire.

It's possible that Sancho Panza's friends thought things might go more smoothly if the squire wasn't let in on the ruse. In any case, when Dorotea appeared in princess garb, Sancho Panza took her for a princess and believed the story that the priest concocted. Dorotea was the Princess Micomicona – come all the way from Micomicón to ask the knight a favor.

Sancho led the way to Don Quixote. The priest and Cardenio followed at a distance, well concealed. By the time our group of friends had found him, Don Quixote'd somehow found his feet. Good luck for all: he was no longer naked. Dorotea could approach Quixote freely and did so as a princess might in books. She dropped down to her knees before the knight and took his hands.

"From this spot I will not rise," she said, "until you grant to me a boon and render me a service. I am the most afflicted damsel the sun has ever shone upon, who has come from distant lands to seek your aid." Storm clouds crossed her pretty face.

"Sir, I am a princess whose kingdom has been stolen by a giant. I beg you, please come with me to Micomicón to conquer him and take my kingdom back. You are my only hope, great knight. Take on my task before all else. I've come so far to kneel before your feet."

It's possible that nothing can restore a knight more quickly than the baleful pleadings of a kneeling princess. And this was such a lovely girl, appearing out of nowhere in the wood in party dress.

Dorotea's sad entreaties did their work.

"Let your great beauty rise," Quixote said, "for I grant whatever favor you would ask of me."

The princess rose. Sancho Panza helped the weary knight back on his horse. "In delay lies danger," said Quixote.

And so the group made off along the trail.

Behind a bush, the priest and Cardenio kept watch. Disguises! More disguises! The priest took his own clothes and cut off his own beard to dress Cardenio. Better that Don Quixote not be reminded of the last time that he and the wild sunburned stranger had crossed paths. They'd come to fisticuffs, you will recall. The priest and costumed Cardenio looked on as the little group of giant killers came their way, and then rushed out to meet them on the trail.

What a coincidence! The priest made quite a show of false surprise. Imagine running into Don Quixote in the wood. So far from home. Out here in the mountains. What good luck!

Reunions and introductions were accomplished – some real and some misleading – and together they set off. They chose a route to Micomicón that would pass by La Mancha on the way.

As the day wore on, the talk was of the princess's dilemma. Dorotea-Princess Micomicona let Quixote in on all the details. Dorotea was a clever girl and conjured up the story as she went.

"My father was a great king, his name was Tinacrio the Sage, so called for knowing what the future held. Among the many things that he foresaw was that he and my mother would die before I'd become old enough to properly defend their throne. Our kingdom would be set on by a giant – a giant from an island near our kingdom. A giant who, to make himself more terrible, would squint and leer and so contort his face to make himself seem cross-eyed. Pandafilendo is his name. Pandafilendo of the Lowering Looking.

"My father said I could agree to marry him and be the leering giant's queen. But if I did not wish a huge and squinting giant for a husband (and he predicted, rightly, I would not), I would have to flee the kingdom to find help. To win our kingdom back from Pandafilendo, I would need to seek a certain knight. His name is Don Azote or Gigote . . ."

"Or Quixote!" sputtered Sancho Panza, marveling at how accurate the fortune-telling king turned out to be.

"That's it," agreed the princess, "Don Quixote."

The king had told her that if the knight should wish it, he could take the princess as his bride, become the king and rule beside her.

Lucky girl with such a choice of husbands: the violent and squinting cross-eyed giant; the stringy and deluded knight with an upturned barber's basin for a hat.

But, once again Don Quixote was duty bound to turn away a princess. He'd never be her husband, he explained. He was promised to the Lady Dulcinea.

The princess took this bravely, but Sancho Panza could not be consoled. To hear the knight refuse this opportunity! He demanded that Quixote think again. How often would Quixote have such chances? He must become a king, for both their sakes.

"Do you think fortune will offer you such luck again? Your Lady Dulcinea is not half as fair. She does not come up to the shoe of this fair princess. Marry! Take the kingdom. It is as though she's been dropped down from heaven. Marry her. Afterward you can have whatever sport you wish with Dulcinea. Lots of kings have something on the side!"

Quixote answered this advice curtly with two blows of his staff to Sancho's head.

But Don Quixote and his squire must have had an appetite to put their fight behind them, or neither was the sort to hold a grudge, for soon Quixote broached a subject one might have thought he would have saved for later.

"Sancho," said Quixote, "for the moment we will put our disagreement to one side. Tell me about your meeting with my lady fair. Leave nothing out in your account. What did you say? What feelings crossed her lovely face as she perused my note? What message would she have passed on to me?

"Perhaps when you encountered her," Quixote said, "she was doing needlework or stringing pearls?"

"No," said Sancho Panza, "she was sieving wheat in the yard."

Sieving wheat? His lady fair? "The grains of wheat must have become white pearls once she had touched them," said the knight.

Don Quixote took another tack. "And when you gave my lady fair my letter did she touch it to her lips to kiss it?" It was a custom of the time to kiss a letter sent by one's beloved.

"No," said Sancho Panza. "She bid me leave it on a sack of wheat. She said she'd maybe get to it when she had time."

"Ah, yes!" said Don Quixote. "The better to enjoy my words at leisure." And did the squire have any other news to tell of his beloved? What else? Was she as lovely as the dawn?

"She's taller than I am by quite a bit," the squire said. "And sweaty." Runny is the word he used. "As runny as a man."

Runny? Dulcinea? Well this did not make sense, but never mind.

But then another question from the knight – ironclad romantic, possessor of a steadfast rosy vision: "And did she give you a precious jewel to give me? That is the custom, I believe."

"No," said Sancho Panza. "But she threw a sheep's cheese overtop the wall as I was leaving. Perhaps the cheese was meant for you. She didn't say."

A cheese! As gift to an absent lover? Such novelty. Utility. Such thoughtfulness.

Romance!

"And you have made this visit very quickly," said the knight. "You must have been transported by a friendly sage!"

⁂

Do you recall the boy whom Don Quixote rescued from a beating early on? Well, here he was again. He came toward our party on the road. He knew his erstwhile savior right away.

The boy rushed toward Don Quixote in a flood of tears and wrapped his arms about Quixote's legs. Quixote knew the boy as well. His heart filled up with tenderness.

He called the boy "my son" and told the other travelers the story of the time they'd met before.

Don Quixote'd saved him from a beating.

Once the boy had mastered his emotions, though, he made it clear his tears were not brought on by gratitude. Instead he was reminded of the suffering the knight had caused. The boy, it seems, had just come out of hospital. He'd been there ever since his meeting with Quixote on the road.

Quixote's interference had so enraged the farmer that he'd thrashed the boy more soundly than he would have if Don Quixote hadn't come along.

Quixote had done the boy no kindness, but the boy now had a boon to ask. If ever Don Quixote might be tempted to offer any sort of help again, would he resist?

"Even if my enemies are chopping me to pieces," said the boy, "I ask you to leave well enough alone. May God curse you and all knights-errant in the world."

An Evening at the Inn;
Don Quixote Fights a Giant in His
Sleep; The Lady in White Robes

@@@@@

We return now to the inn: home of an inn-keeper, his kindly wife, their daughter, and the frisky servant girl Maritornes, cheerful, willing plaything of the muleteers. We reach the place where Sancho Panza had suffered from a blanketing, where Don Quixote had been beaten by a Moor and Sancho Panza by four hundred Moors, where our hero had fended off a lovesick widow.

The barber gave up his disguise. He now appeared his plain old self, pretending to be stunned at the coincidence of meeting at the inn.

This time, the knight agreed to pay for rooms and he was ushered up the stairs to bed. His madness in the hills had made him tired.

Downstairs the other travelers sat down to dinner. At first they talked about Quixote as they ate, and then about the books behind his madness. They were all familiar with the stories, some admitting this and others not. People like to boast they do not share the silly interests of the common herd.

Luckily, the innkeeper was not the type to put on airs. At dinner he regaled his guests with the tales he liked best. He told the story of a knight who took on an army of great soldiers on his own, causing them to run away like bleating sheep.

He told the story of a knight who, sailing on a river, met a flaming serpent. The knight jumped on the monster's back and somehow got his hands around its neck. He strangled it until the beast gave up its life and sank below the waves. The serpent sank, the hero on its back. Down below, the snake became a wise old man, with fascinating secrets to divulge.

And then there was the story of a knight who cut five giants into halves with one great blow, slicing each one cleanly at the waist.

According to the innkeeper these tales were true, though as he said, the world had changed since then.

The night wore on. Finally, while all about the table ate and drank, caught up in their spiraling good cheer, Sancho Panza climbed the stairs.

Why did he climb the stairs? What did he hear? Noises from Quixote's room? He climbed the stairs to look in on his sleeping master. Oh, yes! The squire's instincts served him well, for something was amiss. The knight was sleeping soundly, but he was not in bed. And not only was he out of bed but in the very throes of deadly combat!

In his dreams the knight had ventured to Micomicón. Don Quixote swung his sword, and robbed a fighting giant of his head, cut it from his neck just like a turnip.

In the darkness of the room Sancho saw the floor awash in giant's blood. Somehow he'd been drawn into the dream.

And then Quixote's voice rang out. "Brigand! Villain! Now I have thee! Thy scimitar shall not avail thee!" He carried on like this, in the language giants understand.

Sancho called for help. The travelers rushed up the stairs. There was Don Quixote, sword aloft, wearing nothing but a greasy nightcap and a nightshirt far too short to cover everything that everyone might dearly wish were hidden. The clamor of the conflict filled the room, the passion and the fury of a battleground.

Of course, there was no giant in Quixote's room. Not the living, breathing kind that Don Quixote dreamed up, nor the fallen headless sort that Sancho Panza believed that he had seen. The giant in the room was quite invented.

There were only wineskins, lying conquered, which earlier were filled up with red wine. The blood the squire had seen was wine, of course. The giant's head a wineskin now quite empty.

Enraged that his precious wineskins had been pierced, the innkeeper descended on the sleeping knight and beat him. The barber threw cold water in Don Quixote's face. Sancho Panza searched about the bedroom for the missing giant. The priest, the barber, and Cardenio put the dreaming knight back into bed.

Poor innkeeper. Poor wineskins. Poor knight.

Quixote returned to bed, the travelers resumed their places back downstairs. New guests arrived. The evening did not end with Don Quixote's conquering the wineskin.

⚭

A group of men on horses made their way into the courtyard of the inn. They wore masks to spare their faces from the wear of travel. With them were their servants, who came on foot. And in their midst, on horseback, rode a lady in white robes. From beneath her veil came sighs and sobs and sounds of grief.

Who was this lady dressed in white, whose stricken soul called out beneath her robes? The servants took her from her horse and brought her in to seat her in a chair. Was she a nun? Judging from her long white robes she might have been.

As this cast of characters came in the door, Cardenio – hiding had become his inclination – fled the room to listen from nearby. Dorotea covered up her face, for it had become her habit to conceal herself as well. The others stood their ground to greet the guests. Everyone was curious and gathered close.

Dorotea ventured forward. It was one woman's heartfelt wish to be some sort of solace to another.

"If it should be anything women are familiar with and know how to relieve," she said, "I offer you my help with all my heart."

At Dorotea's words, an angry answer came from underneath the leader's mask. "Do not waste your time to help her. She will not thank you and she will reward your care with lies."

The lady dressed in robes at last found words. From beneath the veil came this rebuttal: "I have never told a lie."

Cardenio – beyond the door – knew that he had heard the voice before. Startled, without meaning to, Cardenio cried out.

The lady in the long white robes heard in his cry a voice she knew as well. She started from her seat. The leader in the mask reached out to stop her. As she rose, her long white veil came loose and fell away.

It was Luscinda, Cardenio's true love!

She looked about the room, her eyes wild in her flawless face. Had she really heard her childhood love?

She rose to seek the owner of the voice, but as she did, the angry leader of the men in masks reached forward to restrain her. He took Luscinda roughly by the shoulders but, doing so, dislodged his mask.

Underneath the mask was Don Fernando!

Coincidence! Coincidence again! How had this come to pass?

Here we have, in one room, Don Fernando and Dorotea, the peasant girl whom he had tricked and had betrayed. Dorotea now reveals her face. Cardenio comes in.

Here we have Luscinda and Cardenio, lovers torn apart by Don Fernando. Two pairs now reunited.

If you, dear reader, are a bit confused, you'll be forgiven. Nor will you be blamed if you are hopelessly confused. Love is confusing in real life as well, but not in quite this way. But onward. This was a very busy night.

How had Luscinda come to be here, covered in the white robes of a nun? And brought here by the bridegroom whom she'd spurned?

Do you remember that she fainted at her wedding and afterward had vanished from the town? She'd found refuge in a convent. Don Fernando had searched for her and found her. She had no wish to see him. But Fernando, as you know, was not the sort to take no for an answer. He'd captured the unhappy girl and stolen her away. And now, here was his chosen bride, reunited with her own choice, young Cardenio.

Don Fernando's face grew red with anger. He had no experience with life's not turning out as he might wish.

Dorotea would step in to save the day. "You cannot be Luscinda's husband," she said. "You are mine." She pulled at Don Fernando's sleeve. Her eyes filled up with tears.

Fernando should remember all the promises he'd made to her, all the liberties he'd taken with his promised wife – with her, his Dorotea. She begged him on her bended knee to remember how he'd loved her once. Truth be told, she loved her somewhat husband.

And though strategies like this almost never work in life, they sometimes do in books. Don Fernando, finally convinced by all her arguments, took his one-time almost wife into his arms.

He saw again how virtuous and beautiful she was – this woman he had wooed with carnivals and gifts and notes and nighttime serenades, how lovely was this girl whom he'd seduced and then ignored and then escaped. They would begin anew as man and wife.

And Dorotea had forgiven him, it seems. To make their ending happy, we must too.

All wept with joy.

All but Sancho Panza. He wept, but wept instead with

worry. Was Dorotea not the princess of Micomicón? What of his destiny as count or king?

There was another knock upon the door. More travelers arrived, more stories were told. Finally the time arrived for bed, except for one who now was rather rested – Quixote.

Don Quixote Falls into a Trap;
New Travelers Arrive

And where was Don Quixote as the others took to bed? Outside. He had taken it upon himself to guard the inn from – giants.

Had there been some giants seen nearby? We can not slow our pace for quibbles.

He mounted Rocinante and embarked upon the watch. He had in mind to take upon himself another task as well. He'd pine for Lady Dulcinea.

Don Quixote sighed. His eyes grew damp. He lifted up his gaze. He begged the moon for news of his beloved, his lady fair. He asked the sun, still making its long journey to the dawn, to send its rays to greet her in the morning. The sun's rays must not kiss her face, he warned. He would be jealous.

Don Quixote leaned upon his staff, upon his horse,

beneath the moon. He let out such doleful sighs he seemed to let his very soul escape.

The other characters inside the inn were sound asleep, except for two.

Do you remember Maritornes – that capering and downward gazing girl? Do you recall the daughter of the innkeeper as well, the girl whom Don Quixote once thought to be a princess whom he had had to gently disappoint? These two were wide awake as was their girlish zest for fun and games.

Guarding, pining on his horse, yearning for his lady in the night, Don Quixote heard a little female voice call out his name. The voice came from a window in the wall above his head, from an opening where hay was pitched out for the mules.

"Señor, Come over here, señor!"

Quixote thought the window was the egress from some high-up splendid palace room. The voice he heard as fluting notes that might come from a princess, no doubt the very one who had once sought him in his bed. Poor thing! She still loved the knight.

And so our hero called up his response. In the kindest way that he could find, he explained that he was Dulcinea's. Love he could not offer her, he said. "Forgive me, noble lady, and retire to your rooms and do not by any further declaration of your longings compel this knight to show himself ungrateful."

Perhaps there was some other gesture he could make. He asked this of the voice up in the window. Perhaps some sort of miracle would do instead of love? Could he retrieve for her a lock of hair plucked from Medusa's head? Or if she had no taste for snakes, would she prefer a ray of sunshine in a jar?

No answer from the princess. Another voice descended. It was Maritornes, companion to her highness, friend to muleteers.

She told the knight there was one thing that he could offer to the princess to console her. He could offer up his hand for her to touch, just briefly. This would help to heal her breaking heart. This would be enough to ease her pain. The princess knew she could not hope for more.

This small thing she would ask even though she'd do so at the risk of her good name. If her father were to hear of this his rage would be so awful he would not hesitate to cut her head clean off.

"Let the villain try!" Quixote said. "For he will not succeed. No father will take up arms against the tender form of his own daughter as long as I have breath within my lungs."

Don Quixote climbed on Rocinante's back. He stood

on tiptoe, stretching out his arm and reached into the window up above him.

"Lady, take this hand," he said. "This hand no other hand of woman has ever touched, not even she who has possession of my entire self. I give it to you that you may observe its handsome sinews, the network of the muscles, the breadth and capacity of the veins, whence you might judge what must be the strength of the arm that has this hand."

Did he expect the touch of royal lips? Did he expect the soft caresses of a pair of slender perfumed royal hands? He did, but found instead the girls tied up his hand with rope. One end they fastened to his hand, the other to a doorknob in the hayloft through the window.

Quixote found himself standing upon Rocinante's back, his outstretched arm inside the hayloft window. If Rocinante were to move he would be left to dangle by the arm.

And so the girls retired for the night.

The knight had been enchanted. Once again.

Quixote called for help. No one could hear. No one came to find him. It was fortunate indeed that Rocinante was not the sort of valiant steed who moved a muscle when he was not bid to.

By dawn the knight was bellowing for help. None came.

But sunrise came, and with it men on horseback. More travelers, well dressed with pistols dangling at their sides.

They cantered to the gates and knocked. They called out for the innkeeper to rise. They needed water for their horses. They needed to be seen to right away!

Well, Don Quixote, tippytoe aboard his horse, did not let his helpless state restrain his tongue. In sternest tones he set about upbraiding these new guests. They had poor manners, making loud demands. How dare they wake the palace with their shouts?

"Withdraw," Quixote yelled, "and wait until it's daylight, and then we shall see whether it will be proper to open to you or not." He glared at them, ferocious, stretched up high, his arm within the window. Skinny figure on a dozing horse.

"If you are the innkeeper," said a man on horseback, "bid them open up the door."

"Do you think," raged Don Quixote, "that I look like an innkeeper?"

Well, he did not. Nor did he look like any other sort of man they'd met before.

Quixote loudly told the men – these clods, these louts – that they were at the gates of a great palace. Inside these walls was royalty, asleep. Quixote yelled, "Withdraw!"

They knocked upon the gates again, this time loud enough to wake the guests.

It was not only the household that was roused to action. So was a horse beneath one of the men – roused to pay a rustic sort of compliment to Rocinante. He made his way to Don Quixote's horse and undertook a frank and unromantic sort of courtship with his nose. Let's not dwell on detail. Rocinante, not one to take offence at friendly gestures, turned about to welcome the advance.

Poor knight. He lost his horse from underneath his feet and dropped. The rope held fast and pain shot through his arm. His wrist was stretched and twisted. Hanging with his toes above the ground, Don Quixote wriggled in midair and yelled with pain. He yelled and flapped and flung himself from side to side.

He screeched and screamed and made enough commotion that darling Maritornes, fearing she'd be punished for her game, leapt out of bed and, rushing to the hayloft, cut him down.

His pride and arm both injured, the knight Quixote jumped upon his horse. Seeking to buff up his tarnished dignity, he rode around in circles calling out, "Whoever shall say that I have been enchanted with just cause, I challenge him. He must come forth to fight."

His challenge wasn't taken up. No one wished to fight him. No one wished to see him or to hear him. They wanted only water for their horses.

DON QUIXOTE CONSIDERS A RESCUE

⟨◯〰〰〰◯⟩

As life and stories teach us, developments in one quarter do not prevent their cropping up in others. As Quixote rode in circles, making threats from high upon his horse, a fuss was getting underway nearby.

It seems two guests – not guests we've met before – had decided to escape the inn before they'd paid.

However, the innkeeper was always on the lookout for such stunts. He tried to stop the guests. They fell upon their host with blows and kicks. They thrashed him as if he were a bunch of harvest corn.

Now, one might think that what happened next would please our knight. The landlady, her daughter, and the servant girl – all three appealed to Don Quixote for his help. Here were damsels in distress. Damsels? Maybe not, but real distress!

"Sir knight!" the daughter-princess cried, "By the virtue

God has given you, help my poor father, for he is being beaten to a pulp."

Quixote had been spoiling for the chance to right a wrong, and here it was!

He listened to the damsels' frantic pleas. There was no doubt the innkeeper was in great need of timely knightly rescue. Fists and shouts were flying at the gate.

Quixote hesitated.

He said he must consider all his duties. Before he could take on their cause, he would obtain permission from the Princess Micomicona. He'd promised he would put her mission first.

"Then, hurry!"

Quixote went in search of Dorotea.

When he returned, the innkeeper was bloodied and abused. The damsels cried and wrung their damsel hands.

"Please save him."

Quixote would lend his mighty arm.

But first there was a problem to consider. "Is it right," he asked himself aloud, "that a knight of my high station should undertake a skirmish with lowly sorts like these departing guests?" In other words, was rescuing the innkeeper from rabble in keeping with his status as a knight?

So careful he'd become in choosing conflicts, this fellow whom we've seen pick fights with sheep!

"It is possible," he said, "that Sancho Panza should be called upon to set this right. It is a squire's place to fight with brutes."

But we will leave this story here. The innkeeper will find someone to save him.

Encounter with the Barber-Surgeon; Don Fernando Takes a Vote; A Visit from the Holy Brotherhood

⟨≈≈≈⟩

The Devil never sleeps, they used to say. Proof of this came riding through the gates.

It was another character our heroes knew. Their past seemed to be circling round to meet them. It was the barber-surgeon from whom Quixote'd won Mambrino's helmet. And Sancho Panza, you'll recall, had kept the saddle from the fellow's horse.

And who was out there in the yard this very morning but our Sancho? The barber-surgeon knew him right away. As fate would have it, Sancho held in his two hands the very saddle.

"Mister Thief!" the barber-surgeon yelled. "Give up my basin and my packsaddle and everything you stole!"

But Sancho – although caught by surprise – was quick to rally to his own defense. He and the knight had won these things in battle, according to the proper knightly rules. Perhaps this lowly, baseborn lout was ignorant of fine and timeworn codes but Sancho Panza wasn't. The barber-surgeon, unconvinced, hurried forth to take his stolen saddle.

What would Sancho Panza do to emphasize his claim? He hit the barber-surgeon on the head.

Another fight! Fists and kicks and flying blood. The inn, this morning, was a lively place. The guests inside came out to watch the brawl. The pair fought tooth and nail across the yard.

In the crowd, of course, was Don Quixote, who stepped forth to comment on the fray. "My squire took the trappings of the horse, and rightly so. He did so with my blessing. As victors we were due the spoils of victory. Furthermore, the saddle that you see is not a saddle. It has been made to seem so by the skills of the enchanters who cast confusion in my path. The saddle is the finery that befits a handsome horse. As to the bowl, it's no such thing. It is the famous helmet of Mambrino."

If they saw fit to disbelieve him, Don Quixote would provide the proof. He stepped between the men and stopped the fight.

"Run, Sancho," said Quixote, "and fetch the helmet that this barber-surgeon calls a basin."

Sancho Panza did as he was told. Brushing off the dust and dirt from fighting, he bustled off and came back with the bowl.

Quixote held the battered basin high above his head for all to see. Mambrino's helmet, right before their eyes.

The barber-surgeon looked around to search the faces of the crowd. "What do you think?" he asked. "How can he say this basin is a helmet?"

The barber-surgeon naturally expected that the crowd would see the thing his way. This was no legendary treasure that knights would need to wear for righting wrongs. It was a barber's basin. Nothing more. And it was his. The knight was either mad or he was lying.

Poor barber-surgeon. Once more he was caught up in a kaleidoscope – a kaleidoscope that soon was turned again.

The other barber – Don Quixote's long-time friend – could not pass up a chance for fun and mischief. "I am a barber too," Quixote's friend announced, "and I was once a soldier in my youth. I know both the supplies that barbers use and all the tools and garb of war as well. I can say that what we have before us is a golden magic helmet. What you are insisting is a lowly saddle is indeed the fancy trappings of a horse."

And so the barber – Don Quixote's friend – buttressed the delusions of the knight. The priest agreed and so did Don Fernando.

But let us turn our eyes to Don Quixote, for on his face there was a look the likes of which we've never seen him wear. When he spoke he had a brand new tone: uncertainty.

Was this equipment packsaddle or trappings? Suddenly Quixote did not know.

On second look, Quixote said, the trappings did have something of the packsaddle about them. Was he addled by enchantment once again? He squinted at the objects in dispute, looked carefully. Gave up.

"The rest of you will have more luck in seeing things for what they are."

Don Fernando stepped in to keep the game of What Is What? in play.

"We'll take a secret vote," he told the crowd, "and find out what these objects really are. Is that thing that Sancho Panza holds a basin or is it instead the helmet of Mambrino? Is it a packsaddle the squire took or trappings?

Don Fernando went about the group to take a secret vote. He put his ear before the lips of each so they might whisper their decision in his ear. He started off the poll with those who knew about Quixote's special form of madness. It turns out they were glad to join the game. "A helmet, not a basin," whispered each and every one of them to Don Fernando. "And trappings."

He only took the votes of Don Quixote's friends and those who knew him so the matter was decided in advance.

The packsaddle was trappings. The basin was the legendary helmet. "So," said Don Fernando, "all are agreed."

But peace did not descend. At the tally of the vote's absurd result, one member of the crowd found he could not keep quiet any longer.

"I won't believe my ears," he said. "Is it possible you all agree to what is absolutely not the case? This is a packsaddle, not trappings. That is not Mambrino's helmet, but a basin. What reason have you all to talk such nonsense? It occurs to me that you must all be drunk."

Don Quixote summoned up an answer we have seen him think appropriate so often. Somehow he had recovered from his bout of indecision, and had regained his footing in his fantasy.

He raised his lance and cracked it on the speaker's skull.

And so another fight ensued – a fight that seemed just for the joy of fighting. The innkeeper rushed off to fetch his sword. Sancho and the barber-surgeon struggled with the packsaddle between them – cursing, sweating, tearing at their treasure, back and forth. Don Quixote slashed and swung his sword. Cardenio and Fernando joined in. The priest cried out. Dorotea was aghast. Luscinda was afraid. The innkeeper's wife got very busy shrieking. The lovely daughter-princess wept and pled. Maritornes howled like an injured beast. Hunchbacked, she was howling at the ground.

Don Fernando knocked down one of the Brotherhood and jumped about upon his fallen frame.

The courtyard of the inn was filled with cries and shouts, shrieks, confusion, terror and dismay, mishaps, sword cuts, fisticuffs, cudgeling, kicks, and bloodshed.

At last it was Quixote who brought the fighting, which he'd started, to an end. "Hold all!" he cried. "Let's all sheath our swords. Let's all be calm!"

"Why do we fight?" he asked the crowd. "We must be enchanted to carry on this way for no good reason." He quoted from chivalric books to make his point. Examples of disputes brought on by nothing but enchantment. Chapter. Verse.

Quixote talked. One by one the warriors paid heed. Panting, sweating, bleeding, they laid down their arms.

⁂

That day, Don Quixote's past would not stay in its proper place behind him. It came to meet him with its greedy grin.

As the vote was underway, three men had joined the

edges of the crowd. These were members of the Holy Brotherhood, the countryside police.

Think back to the day when Don Quixote had freed the galley slaves. Do you recall the man who lost his liberty for love of laundry? The singer and the matchmaker and the fellow who was much too fond of cousins? The old man with the urinary woes?

With the best intentions he had freed them, whatever those intentions might have been. But the consequences Sancho Panza had predicted had now come.

In the calm that followed the pointless little battle in the courtyard, one member of the Brotherhood suddenly remembered a document he had folded in his coat. It was the warrant for the capture of a criminal: a knight called Don Quixote, who had released a chain gang on the road.

The fellow read the document aloud. And there was Don Quixote's clear description. Very tall, very thin, and old. The costume, the companion, and the horse.

The officer laid hands on Don Quixote. It was official business. Quixote would be punished by the crown. Perhaps he'd be a galley slave himself.

And what was Don Quixote's gesture in response? Can you guess?

He reeled about and grappled with his captor. He grabbed the man with all the strength he could. The delusional are often very strong as we have seen. Something in their hearts supplies their arms. And so it was that day with Don Quixote. Turning on the man who dared entrap him, Don Quixote throttled him so heartily – the Brother's tongue a pink and pointing arrow, his eyes pushed out like organ stops – that our hero would have wrung the life from him had not the others rushed to intervene.

The clutching and the staggering and strangling was stopped. The lunatic Quixote was restrained, but the warrant for the knight's arrest still stood. Quixote was the culprit whom the document described, and the country-side police must take him in.

Quixote dropped his arms and took up words to fight. Words would supply what lance would not.

"Come now, base ill-born brood," he said "Do you call it highway robbery to give freedom to those who are in chains? To release the captives, to help the miserable, to revive the fallen, to relieve the needy? Tell me, who was the ignoramus who signed a warrant of arrest against a knight? Who was he who did not know that knights-errant are not bound by your edicts, that their law is their sword, and their only rules their wills? What knight-errant ever paid poll tax, duty, queen's pin money, or king's dues? What tailor ever let him pay to make his clothes? What king did not seat him at his table? What damsel did not love him and did not yield herself up to his pleasure? And lastly, what knight-errant has there been – is there, or will there ever be in the world – not bold enough to give, single handed, four hundred cudgellings to four hundred officers of the Holy Brotherhood if they come in his way?"

His audience was openmouthed. Nonetheless, Quixote's words did work a sort of magic.

His speech was solid evidence that Don Quixote saw the world through lenses all his own – proof to those who heard it that the speaker was not absolutely sane.

His friend the priest now took the members of the Brotherhood aside. He argued that if they did arrest the knight, Quixote would be soon enough released. According to Spanish law, madmen were not punished for their acts. This the Holy Brotherhood considered. They stroked their chins and finally agreed.

And so Quixote won himself his freedom.

He must leave the "castle" right away, the knight announced. There was a squinting giant to be slain. "In delay," Quixote crowed, "there's danger!"

"For who knows, exalted lady," Don Quixote said to Dorotea, "but that your enemy the giant may have learned by now from spies that I mean to end his life. He might be taking steps right now to fortify himself within a castle!"

The sojourn at the inn was at an end. Onward to Micomicón!

But first the mighty knight must take a nap.

DON QUIXOTE ON THE OXCART

D on Quixote slept. And as he slept, the others schemed. They had to find a way to take him home. Lucky chance would play into their hands, lucky chance that took the shape of oxen.

A herd of oxen came by on the road, driven by an ox driver, who had in tow a cart – a cart that he was willing to let out for rent.

Quixote's friends devised a plan. The driver and his oxen would join in and all of them would travel to La Mancha.

The knight's companions built a cage – a sturdy wooden cage just big enough to hold a knight – and fastened it atop the rented cart. It would be Quixote's cabin for the journey. They'd make use of the oxcart and Quixote's firm conviction that he was oftentimes the victim of enchantment.

They dressed up as magicians and enchanters – except for Sancho Panza, who was not let in fully on the plan.

Perhaps, they worried, Sancho might oppose the ruse. Returning to La Mancha would never make the squire into a king.

The conspirators assembled in Don Quixote's room and, as our hero slowly woke, they tied him up.

The knight did not fight his captors. Is this our Don Quixote who is tied up but does not try to escape?

Even in his sleepy state he reasoned that he could not get away. He was enchanted. Plain as day. He knew that he could not defy magicians.

And Sancho? He stood by, taking in the scene and doing nothing. These characters seemed somewhat familiar, but Sancho held his tongue and fists, and watched.

The barber had prepared some lofty words to make the drama come to life, the sort of speech enchanters might well make. He offered his oration in a solemn voice that rose and fell, loud and soft like chanting in service in a church.

"Oh Knight of Mournful Countenance," he said, "let not this captivity afflict you, for this must be for the more speedy accomplishment of the adventure in which you're now engaged. And you," he said, addressing Sancho Panza "most noble and obedient squire that ever bore a sword or wore a beard, be not dismayed to see the flower of knight-errantry carried off this way before your very eyes. For soon, if it so please the Framer of the Universe, you will see yourself raised up to such a height that you will not know yourself, and the promises that your good master has made to you shall come true."

The barber chanted on. He told Quixote that his destiny was to be the husband of the Lady Dulcinea – that she would be "the mother of his cubs".

Don Quixote did not struggle. He let himself be carried down the stairs. Sancho Panza followed, wary and suspicious, but for the moment kept his worries to himself.

All of this is not to say that Quixote didn't have some questions of his own. He'd never read of knights removed on oxcarts. Enchanted knights, as he recalled, were carried off by swift romantic means, swept away in clouds or stolen off in chariots of fire. Often they were taken on some fabulous unheard-of beast, a hippogryph for instance: a winged horse with eagle's head. That sort of thing.

But clever Don Quixote came up with the explanation he required. Perhaps there was a new style of enchantment. Times change. Hippogryphs and chariots might have given way to oxcarts as a way of taking knights from place to place. All this he confided to his squire.

Sancho Panza's mind was not at peace. He could not make these happenings add up. He told the knight he was not sure enchantment was behind these strange events.

For instance, he explained: had the knight not told him that enchanters were not humans but mere visions? They didn't have the substance that real people do. You could not grasp or hold them; they were made of air.

"But these enchanters," said Sancho, "are flesh and bone. I've touched them. And furthermore," he said, pointing as he spoke at Don Fernando, "that one over there smells of perfume. Devils, we all know, smell like the very stinking gates of hell."

Quixote had an answer at the ready. "A devil changes how he looks and smells when he wishes to pretend he's not a devil. Enchantment! And very clever too!"

The time had come to leave the inn. All who had been staying there embraced. They wished each other well. So many things they'd shared, so many joys and sorrows they had seen together. There were good-byes and smiles and shaken hands and promises that they would meet again.

Quixote and his little band of escorts left the inn. First the oxcart and its owner bearing Don Quixote, captive, tied both hand and foot, accompanied by oxen – the brand new style of moving knights about. Beside the cart, the members of The Brotherhood, with guns. Behind was Sancho Panza and his ass. The two of them were leading Rocinante. Finally, the priest and barber on their mules.

They creaked and rumbled, trudged and rolled along the dusty road toward La Mancha.

Encounter with the Canon
of Toledo; Sancho Voices
His Suspicions

∽◌∾

They had traveled some distance when six or seven men rode up behind them. They were well dressed and riding handsome horses. They seemed to have important business waiting. But they could not resist inquiring about our ragtag band of friends.

Remember that our characters were mostly in disguises that one would seldom see out on the road. And they had a captive on a cart – a somewhat rump sprung figure from a storybook trapped in a cage.

The leader of the group slowed his horse. He was, he said, the Canon of Toledo.

A Canon's an official of the church. As such, he was quite comfortable with asking into other men's affairs. "Who is your prisoner," he asked. This desperado: old and thin and dry and lying still.

The Canon asked The Brotherhood, but it was Don

Quixote who responded. Perhaps his little nap and then his rest within the cage had given our good knight a second wind.

"I am a knight at the mercy of enchanters. They assail me out of envy, but they will not defeat me in the end. I am not the sort of knight who will vanish from the memory of men, but the sort who will be famous all through time. An example for all knights who follow after, whose footsteps will guide them to whatever pinnacles of greatness they might someday reach."

The priest – Quixote's friend – chimed in. He told the Canon, whose expression was perhaps a little skeptical, that everything Quixote said was true.

"This is the Knight of Mournful Countenance," he said, "whose great deeds shall be inscribed on brass and marble, notwithstanding all the efforts of the jealous to obscure them. No matter what the evil do to hide them."

The Canon of Toledo must have wondered if he was awake or dreaming. Briefly he was at a loss for words.

But Sancho Panza, so it seems, was not. "Hold everything," he said. "I think that things are not just as they appear." He'd speak his mind, said Sancho. He was convinced he'd waited long enough.

Had Don Quixote truly been enchanted? Sancho Panza said he was not sure.

Sancho Panza offered up his thinking. "If Quixote is enchanted, he would not eat; he would not sleep. Furthermore, he would not speak; enchanted people usually do not. But if Quixote is not stopped he will talk on and on like thirty lawyers. Enchanted?

"And what is more," said Sancho, turning to the priest – Quixote's friend – becoming more convinced of his own arguments with every passing word, putting other pieces of the puzzle into place as he went on, "Do you think I do not know you in your costume?"

The characters had seemed all too familiar all along.

He continued, "Let it be on your conscience, priest, that you are stopping this great knight from enacting his great feats throughout the world. Let it be on your conscience too, that you prevent me from achieving my own destiny. I'd be a count by now if not for you. My children's father would now be a governor, my wife might be the consort of a viceroy!"

Worrying that Don Quixote might be persuaded by the squire's speech, the priest took the Canon of Toledo to one side. He told this man of God the truth: Quixote had been driven mad by reading books of chivalry. He described the plan they had prepared to take him safely home.

The group moved on, the Canon and his men now among them. They came upon a pasture with grasses for the oxen and peaceful shade for all of them to take their lunch.

But Sancho was not mollified by thoughts of lunch alone. Is this our same old Sancho?

His arguments had still not been addressed. As they came near the resting place, the squire found a moment to approach Quixote's cage. He spoke to Don Quixote, squire to knight. "These captors are not enchanters. They are friends and people from the inn. That is the priest, right there. There is your friend, the barber. They are doing what they can to stop our mission. They envy you because you are a knight."

Sancho Panza told the knight that he could prove this. Quixote had to answer one quick question.

Don Quixote spoke with patience to his squire. "It is possible," the knight explained, "these captors look like people whom we know, but enchanters take whatever form they like. They've taken on the shape of friends so that we'll think they are friends and not magicians."

How often need Quixote spell this out?

"And furthermore," Quixote said, "if I am not enchanted, how is it I am trapped within a cage upon a cart? Such things never happen to great knights. Impossible! What seems to be, quite simply is not so.

"As to the question that you'd like to ask me, ask and I will answer if you like."

Sancho Panza asked Quixote this: "Since you have been shut up in the cage, have you felt at all the urge to . . . have you needed to do the sort of thing that . . . how can I put this nicely? . . . can not be put off to another day?"

Don Quixote did not understand. What sort of thing could not be put off for later?

Sancho tried again. "I am speaking of that thing that no one else can do on your behalf."

"What," wondered the knight, "could that thing be? No one can do on my behalf? What thing?"

Finally, the great knight understood what Sancho could not bring himself to say out loud.

"Why, yes," said Don Quixote, "I have needed to and need to do that very thing right now!"

Sancho pressed on. "Have you never heard it said," he asked Quixote, "'I do not know what ails this man? He neither eats not drinks nor sleeps. You'd think he was enchanted?' Well, you not only eat and drink and sleep and talk as much as thirty lawyers, but furthermore you have the most commonplace of functions to perform! Have you heard of enchanted people with these needs?"

Don Quixote still was not convinced. "I must perform these functions!" said Quixote. "But this might be some new form of enchantment. Perhaps these things are now among the functions of a captive knight.

"And furthermore I have another proof that I'm enchanted: if I were not it would be weighing on my conscience that I am languishing all day within this cage, depriving the world of all my skills and courage."

Sancho Panza would not be put off. He was determined that the knight should leave his cage.

"Look at Rocinante, so sad without his master on his back. Why don't we try our luck at more adventures. If things don't work out well, you can go back in your cage. And this time I will join you."

And so the knight agreed to his release.

The squire raised the matter with the priest. The captors must permit the knight, for decency and cleanliness and for the sake of all their many noses, to leave his cage. Sancho Panza said that he would guarantee that Don Quixote would not run away.

Quixote gave his word as well. "I can not get away, even if I wish to. I am enchanted." Whoever had enchanted him could freeze him in position at their will. What chance had he to flee? Why even try? He would come flying back, right through midair, flying backward, upright as he stood.

And so Quixote was set free. He stood and stretched with pleasure. He went to Rocinante and offered him a pat and friendly word – his dear and faithful horse. "Oh flower of all steeds," he said, "we shall see ourselves, both of us, following the calling for which God sent me out into the world."

But onward, on a mission to the bushes! There was a calling besides God's that he must answer.

He came out of the scrub a man reborn.

The Glory that Is Chivalry

The Canon of Toledo had watched the knight conduct all these decisions and debates. He asked himself a question many who had known the knight had asked before. How could a man so eloquent, keen-witted in some ways, be so unhinged on one subject alone: the books of chivalry. He only lost his stirrups when the subject of his favorite books was broached.

As Quixote joined the group, the Canon had some questions for the knight.

"Is it possible that you can really think yourself a knight? Is it true the things you've found within these books have made you truly think you are enchanted? Do you believe in monsters and in giants and the stories of the battles and the dwarves and in squires who will someday become counts or even kings? Is it possible that by merely reading all these books you have been reduced to such condition that you must be locked in a cage, taken place to place as though you are a wild beast?"

Even with his mind a little clouded with enchantment, these questions struck an unexpected and unnerving chord in Don Quixote.

"It seems to me," said Don Quixote, reeling from the Canon's inquisition, "you believe the stories that one reads in books of chivalry are false!"

"That's true," replied the man of God. "For myself, I can only say that when I read them, so long as I do not stop to think that they are lies, they give me a certain pleasure. But when I come to think of what they are, I fling the very best of them against the wall."

"If you think these books are lies," Quixote said, "perhaps you'd like to argue that the sun does not shine light. That ice is never cold. That the earth beneath our feet does not sustain us."

And then Quixote found another sort of argument to make, based more on human nature than on nature.

"How can you not believe these tales," he asked the man of God, "when doing so would bring you so much joy?" Would you not be happier believing in the world as it exists and is described within these books?"

Dreamily, Quixote embarked upon a story, the sort

of tale that shows a world according to the gospel that is chivalry.

"We see before us a lake," said Don Quixote

"It's filled not with water but with blackest pitch. It is a lake of bubbling pitch and swimming in this rolling blackness there are serpents, there are lizards, there are monsters. Our knight looks on this terrible expanse: filth and horror, terror, danger, stench – all in a deathly stew.

"And then he hears a voice as if from nowhere. A lonely voice. Our hero listens closely. No, it is not from nowhere. It comes – he knows this in his heart – from somewhere hidden deep within the lake.

"The voice commands, 'Knight, who sees this dread lake, if thou would win the prize that lies beneath these dusky waves, prove the valor of thy heart and cast thyself into its dark and burning waters, else thou shalt not be worthy to see the mighty wonders contained in the seven castles down beneath this black expanse.'

"What is the knight who hears this to do? Stopping only long enough to speak the name of his beloved lady, he throws himself into the darkness of the monster-ridden lake of burning pitch. So brave is he.

"But does he find his death among the waves? He does not. He does not drown, is not destroyed by beasts. His goodness and nobility have won him passage to a kingdom underneath the waves. Goodness and nobility are given due reward in books like these.

"Back to our knight. Underneath the waves are flowered meadows beneath a cool blue sky and groves of trees with brightly colored birds that jump and flit among the leaves. The knight drops under water to a paradise.

"He finds a brook with pebbles made of gold and pearls. He finds a fountain spouting colored waters and then another, made of crystal and green jewels. They look like they are emeralds. Probably they are.

"And then the knight sees a golden castle with ornaments of pearls and gold and precious gems. He ventures forth. Birdsong, jewels, and dancing waves above. And whom should he encounter at the castle gates? Emerging from this castle there are damsels. They have been sent to greet him in costumes of such opulence, they could only be described as indescribable.

"The fairest of the damsels takes him by the hand and brings the knight inside. She takes away his clothes. She bathes him with precious soaps and oils and dresses him in the softest, richest garments, sprinkled with perfumes. She drapes him with a mantle said to be worth at least a city. She leads him to a chamber and seats him on a chair carved out of ivory. There are more lovely girls to serve him. They offer him a banquet so magnificent that he can not decide what he should eat. Finally, he chooses.

"All the while there's music. Who is singing? Who is playing? He does not know. Pleasure has been offered to his every sense.

"When the meal is over, the knight leans back and picks his teeth. This shows that he is comfortable, at ease. The many lovely girls sigh with relief.

"The knight looks up. Another door is opening. Another damsel comes into the room. If such a thing were possible, she is more beautiful than all the damsels he's already seen. She comes toward the knight. She sits beside him, leans toward our hero."

And what will happen next?

"Read these books," said Don Quixote, "Read these books and they will drive the sadness from your soul. They have from mine. And since I have taken up believing in these books," he said, "I have become more brave, better mannered, more tolerant, polite, and generous – more thoughtful and more patient in my many trials. Not only that, but now that I'm a knight myself – now that I have taken these great works as my example – I have the chance to be an emperor or king and ensure the elevation of my squire as well."

The world of chivalry: paradise and joy. Goodness that will end in a reward.

The lunch was brought and spread out on the carpets. The travelers stretched out upon the ground.

The Rescue of the Virgin Mary; The Knight Is Dealt a Dreadful Blow

⎰⎰⎰

Our characters enjoyed a pretty picnic in the grass. They were more fortunate than some, for it had been a hard year in this part of Spain. There had been very little rain.

When times were hard, processions ventured forth on holy journeys, taking to the roads to make their way to holy sites to ask the Lord above to show them kindness. God would look down on them, poor suffering believers, calling up to Him to show His mercy, and He would send the rain. Or so they hoped.

Such was the group that now came down the road, preceded by the doleful notes of trumpets – several men, all dressed in white. Some of them were chanting and beating at their naked skin with whips. Others carried above their heads a statue of a figure dressed in black. It was the Virgin Mary, held high to capture God's attention.

Did the Virgin capture God's attention? How can we know? We do know that she captured Don Quixote's. To Don Quixote, she seemed to be – you'll never guess! – a lady fair. To Don Quixote's eyes this dark unmoving lady had been kidnapped and she was being held against her will.

Oh, his companions warned him! Quixote's friends did what they could to stop him from meting out his own misguided justice. His friends called out that this was not a damsel in distress. To no avail.

Quixote jumped upon his horse and cantered forth to meet the line of penitents. Reaching them, he asked them to explain to him what they were doing with this lady on the road.

Ordinary travelers don't like to be waylaid. How much more true this was of travelers whose plan it was to whip their flesh until their trip was done! The penitents did not wish to be slowed.

But Don Quixote would not let them pass. "You will release your captive," he said. "Unhand the damsel in distress."

The penitents could not believe their ears.

Despite their solemn hearts, despite the flaying of their flesh and year of drought, the penitents broke out in hearty laughter.

Enraged, Quixote lifted up his lance to strike a blow.

But one among the penitents brought up his staff as well, and landed it so heavily on Don Quixote's shoulder that the knight was knocked from off his horse and dashed upon the ground.

And there he lay.

Don Quixote moved not hand nor foot. He showed no sign of life. No more so than the Virgin, whose sightless eyes gazed off above their heads.

Wind and sun and silence.

Could just one blow have in one moment killed the knight? No. It was not possible. And yet, perhaps it had. Things that are not possible do happen, and happen all the time.

Suddenly the empty air was filled with cries.

Sancho, ran to where his master lay. "Don Quixote!" he cried out. "My master! He is a man who's never done an injury to any living creature." (If ever there were a proper time to bend the truth a little this was it). He crouched over his master and then reached down to hold him in his arms.

The penitent who struck the blow lifted up his skirts and ran away. Ran like a deer. Ran like the blowing wind. Ran from the place where he'd become a murderer.

Quixote did not stir. No person moved.

The Virgin kept her eyes on the horizon.

Did God look down and see his tiny subjects?

Sancho Panza, eloquent in grief, sent his sorrows

upward to the skies. "Oh flower of chivalry," he cried, "that one blow should have ended your well-spent life! Oh pride of all La Mancha. Pride of all the world, that for want of you will be full of evildoers, no longer in fear of punishment for their misdeeds! Oh great Don Quixote, humble with the proud, haughty with the humble, encounterer of dangers, endurer of outrages, imitator of the good, scourge of the wicked – in short, knight-errant, which is all that can be said."

Thus, Sancho Panza called out the contents of his breaking heart. Louder. Louder. He bellowed out his grief and wept above his master's fallen form. In fact, so loud did Sancho wail and keen, he managed something no doctor or enchanter could. He managed to revive the fallen knight.

"Sancho Panza, help me climb into the cage, for I have not the strength to mount my horse," said Quixote.

"This I will do with all my heart, Señor. Let us make our way now to our village. There we will prepare for another sally, which may turn out more profitable than this."

"It would be wise," Quixote said, "to let the evil influences of the stars that now hold sway pass by."

He was alive, and he was asking for captivity.

Don Quixote took his place within the cage upon the cart. The Officers of The Brotherhood decided they were no longer needed. The Canon, extending all good will, was on his way as well.

Returning home at last were Don Quixote, his friends the priest and barber, Sancho Panza, and the faithful Rocinante, and the ass.

The journey to their village took six days.

THE STORY ENDS

It was Sunday when the troop arrived. The oxcart rolled into the square, bearing Don Quixote in his cage. He was thinner than the townsfolk gathered there remembered, and yellow with disease.

How glad they were to have him home that day. He was almost the famous knight he'd once described to Sancho, arriving at the foreign far-off castle.

Two boys ran off to fetch Quixote's housekeeper and niece. Sancho Panza's wife hurried out into the square to welcome Sancho Panza and to squabble and complain, to embrace him and to ask what he had brought for her. She was relieved to see their ass was safe as well. Laugh at their affections if you will, but these two loved their donkey very much.

Sancho, in the village square, told his wife a little of his travels. He told her knightly ventures oftentimes don't turn out as one hopes. He took pains to describe his dreadful blanketing. "Still," he said, "Nothing in the world is finer than to be the squire of a knight-errant and a seeker of adventure. It is a fine thing to be on the lookout for what might happen next: crossing mountains, searching woods, climbing rocks, visiting castles, putting up at inns. Freedom and nothing to be paid." And he told her that the next time out, he would return a governor or king!

This was good news for Sancho Panza's wife. But, best of all, her husband had come home! He'd been gone, she said, "for centuries."

In Don Quixote's household there was the bustling of the women, the practical effects of love and worry. They led him to his room, took off his clothes, and laid their tired master on his bed.

From beneath half-opened lids, Don Quixote watched them with suspicion and confusion. Who were they, these very kind and fussy creatures? Broken, ill, and just as mad as ever, Quixote did not know the time and place.

On that day, the priest predicted Don Quixote's fate. His body would be well again, he said. Otherwise his future was unclear. Quixote's mind was spinning, still imagining the stuff of storybooks. The figure in the bed was still a knight.

Sending up their curses on the works of chivalry, the women took on Don Quixote's care, shrugging onto their shoulders the mantle of anxiety they would henceforth wear. It is the price that one must pay for love – the price that women pay with daily duty.

And so we leave our hero on his bed, in his bedroom in La Mancha, nursed and coddled by his housekeeper and niece. They straighten sheets. They offer soup. For now they have the chance to keep him safe.

Epilogue

W hat would happen to the knight when he was well? Whatever would become of Don Quixote the ingenious *hidalgo* of La Mancha? Brave and foolish Don Quixote. The knight who was so kind and yet so dangerous, clever and ridiculous, deluded, wise and sweet, violent and good, quick of temper, pure of heart, confused.

Was he truly mad? Or was he not? How much did Don Quixote really know about the workings of the world that reeled around him?

The story's, for the moment, at an end.

Cervantes gives us only clues of Don Quixote's future. He tells us of some scraps of papers found beneath the ruins of a chapel – sealed up in a buried leaded box. He says these papers came to light long after Don Quixote met his death.

According to the papers, and to the legends of La Mancha, Don Quixote took to the road again. He went to Saragosa for the jousting – games played using horses at full gallop and with spears.

There were more adventures for the knight. Another sally.

But these are stories for another book. Cervantes would take up his pen again.

Cervantes? What became of him? He died four hundred years ago. They say he had a child who had no children.

Time has pulled its veil around Cervantes, and, for now, around Quixote too.

Quixote, or Quixada, or Quexana. We do not know his name. He could be anyone. Any soul upon this spinning Earth. Cervantes. Don Quixote. You or me.

We draw the curtains here. We leave Quixote, home at last, weak, but gaining strength upon his bed.